DYLAN THE ROGUE

A WOLF SHIFTER FATED MATES PARANORMAL ROMANCE

BILLIONAIRE WOLVES SERIES
BOOK EIGHT

CHARMAINE LOUISE SHELTON

CONTENTS

ABOUT DYLAN THE ROGUE: A WOLF SHIFTER FATED MATES PARANORMAL ROMANCE

A tough wolf shifter who doesn't believe in fated mates walks into a diner and his knees buckle. Yeah, tell me about it...

I fought my best friend to challenge him for Alpha of the Billionaire Wolves of Miami pack run by his family for millennia. The same prince of the pack who befriended me when we were pups because others taunted me for being the lowest ranking member.

So, no, I don't give a damn about others. I've had to put myself first my entire life. And now, I'm a lone wolf. I use my brawn—and my wolf senses—to win in underground fight clubs. Nothing and no one make me weak. Until her. Sasha Volkov. The jagged scar on her face can't mar this beauty.

I'm a waitress in a nondescript diner in New York City. A place I hide from my pack. The Alpha and his followers profit when they force unclaimed she-wolves to breed then sell the pups on the underground market. And I was next.

I thought I'd escaped others of my kind. Then a beast of a male Dylan Vang walks into the diner, and my wolf leaps for joy. But I can't let anyone find me, not even my fated mate.

*Their steamy love story is a standalone in the sizzling **Billionaire Wolves Series** of interconnecting stories featuring wolf shifter fated mates romance. Get a glimpse of their dynamism in other books.*

Anthem: "By Your Side" Sade
https://www.youtube.com/watch?v=C8QJmI_V3j4

Visit CharmaineLouiseBooks.com

CHAPTER 1

Four Years Ago — The Everglades, Florida
Dylan

"WE CELEBRATE two momentous occasions today! The return of my eldest son Jagger to our pack after his graduation from Duke University magna cum laude with a Bachelors of Arts in economics and an MBA. He will take over as CEO of Larson Enterprises, Inc. I step down as your Alpha and the head of our company after decades of unprecedented success—"

Wolf whistles, stomping feet, and cheers fill the steamy air of the Everglades as members of the Miami Wolves Pack applaud our leader and his eldest son's accomplishments. Also known as the Billionaire Wolves of Miami since we're the most powerful pack in the South.

Several millennia ago, Scandinavian Viking wolf

shifters sailed from the Old World and landed along the East Coast of what's now the United States. The six packs headed by best friends who sought new lands moved throughout the continent to form territories, with ours settling here. We maintain close ties with the others through relationships—mating and business. Plus, the Ruling Council gatherings keep packs informed of happenings throughout the wolf shifter world.

I ignore those around me as my gaze focuses on Jagger.

The pack prince and wannabe Alpha grins as he basks in the members' adoration. At twenty-four, he's a year younger than me. His ice blue eyes sparkle in the brilliant sun. The golden light hits his short white blond hair as though the gods themselves anoint him with their favor. The same six feet, seven inches as me, muscular but with less brawn. His biceps flex as he catches the she-wolf Melissa—his on-and-off lover—who launches herself at him. Possessive bitch.

Her giggles as she plasters Jagger's face with wet kisses reach me, where I stand at the back of the crowd. She clings to him like a baby monkey, with her arms and legs wrapped around his neck and hips tightly. She bounces up and down as though riding his cock.

The other she-wolves who vie for Jagger's attention—who doesn't want the pack prince?—grumble and roll their eyes at Melissa's overdone theatrics. Not that I blame them. She's tried to lay claim to Jagger for years. Even going so far as to thwart other potential mates during multi-pack runs and fancy balls where the females paraded themselves before Jagger. The rest of us? Unworthy.

The thoughts make me growl. Those nearby glance at me nervously. They're right to be concerned and to shuffle away. I'm known for my bristly attitude. *The Beast* as they call me. I glare back and fold my arms across my massive chest while my stance widens. Muscles chiseled from years of MMA training bulge beneath my black t-shirt and low-slung faded jeans. The lightning bolts from the pack tattoos ripple along my arms from shoulders to wrists. I crack my knuckles to mimic the staccato of lightning.

I shift my gaze back to the front where Jagger stands next to his father, with Melissa by his side. His younger brother, Viggo, and best friends, Tag Dahl and Rust Ingolf, flank Jagger. He glances around the crowd, more than likely seeking me out.

At one time, I would have been beside him as his fourth best friend.

"You fucking loser, Dylan!"

Punch to my stomach. My hands wrap around my midsection as I grit my teeth and bear the pain.

"Yeah! Just like your old man!"

Slash to my back by jagged claws ripping through my t-shirt into my flesh. I bite back a yowl.

"You need to get the hell out of our pack! We don't want thieves like your lot around!"

Kick to my knee. I drop to the other one and glare up at my attackers through angry tears as I commit each face to memory. Then my head snaps back with a sharp crack.

"And where is your father, huh? I bet he's living it up on our pack's money!"

Kick to my head, and I curl into a defensive ball on the damp grass in the Everglades. My arms cover my vulnerable head and neck as their vicious assault continues. Uncountable blows hit my sore body as the young wolves, driven by their hate whale on me. Alone and smaller than them, I can only lie there and take it.

"What the fuck do you think you're doing?!"

The blows stop immediately. Silence descends. Tension runs high.

"I said, 'What the fuck do you think you're doing?!'"

Firm hands lift me to a seated position.

I open one puffy eye and squint towards the voice I recognize even without sight. Jagger Larson—the Alpha's oldest son. He's a year younger than me. But unlike me, he commands the older males. I squint around. They cast their wary eyes down in submission. Their leader mumbles a response, and Jagger growls deep in his chest. They shrink under his disapproval.

"Your behavior does not demonstrate how our pack treats members. If I catch or hear of you attacking another one of us, you will answer to me. Do you understand?"

The males cave into themselves as they mutter their agreement. Then they turn tail when Jagger dismisses them. I watch him as he watches their hasty retreat. A flicker of happiness sparks in my heart. But I tamp it down.

Jagger gazes down at me and extends his hand.

I scowl at it, then at him, and stagger to my feet. He grasps my upper arm to steady me, and I shrug it off with a growl.

"Hey. No need to thank me for saving your ass. Dylan,

right?" *Jagger says with a smirk as he folds his arms over his chest. "Would you rather I left you to fend for yourself?"*

"Fuck off, Jagger. It's not the first time, and I can take it. Without your help," I respond with a snarl as my golden eyes flash. My wolf prowls just below the surface.

Jagger chuckles and shakes his head. Long white blond hair falls into his ice blue eyes. He claps me on the back and guides me towards our pack's camping ground.

"I'm sure you can. But why should you face them alone when you can have backup?"

I jerk out of his grip and spin to glare at him.

"No need to brag, Daddy's boy. They only listen because your father is our Alpha."

He studies me for a moment, then shrugs, unruffled.

"Perhaps. Perhaps not. But the point is, they left you alone. I get why you're pissed, Dylan. Hell, I would be too if my father left my mother pregnant with me and stole money from our pack, leaving us to face bullies."

He raises his hands, palms out in surrender, when I snarl and bare my fangs. My wolf leaps to the forefront. We do not take kindly to anyone speaking ill of my mother.

"Listen, just saying I get your anger and hurt, Dylan," he says then cocks his head towards the camping grounds. "Viggo, Tag, Rust, and I head for a run. You're welcome to join us. In your wolf form, you'll heal faster."

I eye him skeptically but find no guile. It's time I have some friends, I think as I nod.

He claps me on the back again, and we return to the camping grounds in companionable silence.

From that day on, the five of us have been inseparable. Jagger including me with his high-ranking brother and friends elevated my status within the pack. Never again did anyone use me as a punching bag or make snide comments about my mother and me being omegas—the lowest ranking members of the pack.

But then Jagger left the pack for selfish reasons and things changed. He doesn't deserve to lead our pack.

I shake my head to clear thoughts from the past, to focus on the future—my future.

"Does anyone challenge Jagger as the next Alpha of the Miami Wolves Pack?"

The laughter and chatter drop to a hush as Alpha Marcus casts his ice blue gaze around the crowd. Older and stronger male wolf shifters shake their heads in denial. They step back to emphasize no desire to challenge the pack prince. Then the Alpha's steely gaze lands on me.

"I challenge Jagger Larson as the next Alpha of the Miami Wolves Pack."

All heads swivel in my direction, including Jagger's, as his mouth opens in surprise. He closes it quickly and pins me with an intense stare. In his eyes, emotions flicker from shock to doubt to irritation. But he remains composed. Unlike his father, who sputters.

"Dylan Vang, *you* challenge Jagger?" He asks gobs-macked. His eyes flit to his son's impassive face and back to my determined one.

Erik—the pack's Beta—growls as though insulted by my declaration.

"I do," I respond as I stride forward through the crowd. The members part, stepping away from me as though I'm contaminated with silver. I ignore them. Eyes focused on Jagger.

My mother Lena touches my arm as I pass her. I shake my head, and her fingers clutch at me.

"Dylan, don't. Please!"

I glance down at her. Green eyes beg me. Undoubtedly, she doesn't want to face harsh scrutiny and possible banishment again should I lose.

My mother never remarried or bore another pup. Instead, she works in the principal's office of the packs' school on Moon Island—our private island in Biscayne Bay. She says the pups there are all she needs, aside from her son.

"Dylan—"

"Mother, do not worry," I tell her as I pry her fingers from my forearm. She sobs and lowers her gaze in defeat.

I stride forward and stand before Alpha Marcus.

"I will not question why you would challenge your best friend, as it is the right of any member of our pack who wishes to lead," he says gruffly. Gone is the man who treated me like a son after my own father abandoned me. But I have my reasons. He lifts his gaze to the pack. "Make room for the challenge."

The members murmur amongst themselves as they move to form a circle in the center of the pack's camping grounds.

"What the fuck, Dylan?!"

I flick my gaze to Viggo. He stares at me in disbelief.

"For real, Dylan?" Rust asks, anger in his hazel eyes.

Tag shakes his head in disgust and folds his arms over his solid chest.

I ignore them and focus on Jagger, who doesn't speak a word.

He steps forward and passes me to enter the circle. He reaches behind his head to yank his t-shirt off by the collar and tosses it aside. Melissa scoops it up and hisses at me.

"He never should have befriended you, Dylan!" She snarls as her amber eyes flash with her wolf.

Jagger's mother, Sigrid, and younger sister Signy watch me as I pivot. Their disappointed gazes give me pause. But I shake them off. Focus, Dylan.

My shoulders square as I crack my neck. Then yank my t-shirt overhead.

"Male or wolf?" Alpha Marcus asks when I step into the circle.

I glance at Jagger, who remains stoic.

"Male," I respond.

Alpha Marcus flicks his gaze between Jagger and me and nods. "The challenge ends when one yields to the other. The fate of the loser rests with the victor. Begin!"

He steps away. A tense silence descends on the pack. Even the insects cease their buzzing. A barred owl flies overhead. It's said if you encounter one during the day, it lets you know you're on the path to enlightenment. Good news will change your life. How appropriate.

Jagger and I circle each other, gauging the best moment to lash out.

I call on my MMA training and attack with an unexpected double-leg takedown to sweep him from his feet. Then I pounce to grapple him into a submission hold. The dexterity of his wolf allows him to roll away and leap to his feet. I snarl and regroup.

He comes at me with a knee strike, followed by successive jabs to my ribs. I stumble back. He advances. We continue to spar with calculated, forceful moves. A human could never withstand the blows. But our wolves make us more powerful and harder to take down with ease. Finally, I get Jagger in a clinch hold.

"Yield, dammit!" I growl.

He relaxes in my grip.

"You want to run off to Duke just to get away from the she-wolves who want you to claim them as your mate? For real, bro?! You have to be kidding me," I say to Jagger as we sit on the beach in front of his family's bayfront mansion on Moon Island.

In the morning, he flies on their private jet to North Carolina and leaves his responsibilities to the pack behind. How privileged.

"You wouldn't understand, Dylan," he responds as he tosses back the last of his beer and drops it in the paper bag..

Of course, he'd think I'm too dumb to understand his reasons. I grunt and finish my beer, then crumple the can one fisted. I toss it into the bag and pull out another.

"Don't you think you owe it to your family's pack to stay here, claim your mate, and wait to become Alpha when your father steps down?"

Jagger runs his fingers through his newly cropped hair—another change he insisted he needed to make. Then sighs in frustration.

"Listen, I don't want to talk about it. I just want to enjoy the last night with my boys."

"But—"

"Hey, hey, hey! Let's get this party started!"

We turn at Rust's words. He strides over with Viggo and Tag. Behind them, Melissa and a few she-wolves wave. Their lush bodies ripe in tiny string bikinis.

Jagger's shoulders rise with tension at the sight of them. He mumbles under his breath as Melissa bounces past the others and drops onto his lap. Over her shoulder, he stares grimly at the bay.

He just doesn't get how lucky he is or the struggles others face. He doesn't deserve to lead the pack...

"Fuck you, Dylan."

Jagger's growl snaps me back to the present as he flips over and grips me in a powerful chokehold. Flat on my stomach with my neck trapped in the crook of his elbow while his other arm pulls back to tighten his grip, white lights flash before my eyes. His knees press my arms into the grass. My legs flail to gain purchase.

"Yield, damn you!" Jagger snarls and closes off more of my air supply. "Yield. Now!"

His Alpha command forces my body to give in.

I deflate beneath him, unable to fight his power. Centuries of Alpha blood in his veins make him the stronger of us. I hadn't considered that ability in my quest to challenge him for leadership. Again, brawn and no brain.

"Yield," I wheeze.

Instantly, he jumps to his feet and stalks from the circle. Wild cries rise as the pack follows him. Chants of Alpha Jagger fill the air. I'm left gasping for breath in the dirt. Only my mother remains. In silence, she kneels beside me and dabs my bloody and sweat-drenched face with my t-shirt.

"Dylan Vang, our Alpha Jagger demands your presence in the clubhouse now."

I glance up to find Tag above me. I nod and rise. Pain shoots through my battered body. My mother sobs softly and pats my arm. I turn to her and pull her into a tight embrace. She shudders and squeezes me back.

We enter the clubhouse. She refuses to leave my side as I approach Jagger on the platform. He stares at me once more with an impassive expression.

"Dylan Vang, you challenged me for Alpha of the Miami Wolves Pack, and you lost. I cast you out as a member and ban you from our entire territory."

My mother gasps and trembles. I squeeze her hand to reassure her without taking my eyes from Jagger. He continues.

"You have twenty-four hours to leave. I will tell the other five Alphas you are a rogue wolf who challenged his Alpha and former best friend. If you enter their territories, you must meet with them for permission to stay. It will be up to them whether they allow you or forbid you. From this day forward, I will have nothing to do with you, Dylan Vang. Leave my presence. Go."

Jagger pivots to give his back to me.

The rest of the pack follow their new leader and shun me. Only my mother walks beside me as I leave the clubhouse.

Once again, the barred owl flies overhead.

My life has changed forever.

CHAPTER 2

Two Months Ago — Rural Pennsylvania
Sasha

"YOU DARE to run away again, Sasha Volkov?! And to take two other she-wolves with you?! Now one of them is dead. You have been here long enough to know better. You will pay for your disobedience."

A violent shiver courses through me while the pack Alpha Kirill *Our Lord* Gusev towers over me. I kneel at his feet in the dirty straw strewn across the floor of the dilapidated barn.

The place of nightmares where he and his henchmen lock the pack's unclaimed she-wolves of breeding age in the grungy stalls lined with silver to prevent them from escaping. Kirill forces the she-wolves to breed with him and his rabid followers, then sell the pups on the underground market. The value of she-wolf pups ranges high since many packs lack females.

Almost a year passed since the night a group of male wolf shifters raided my original pack's land outside of St. Petersburg in Russia. I awoke to terrified screams and savage snarls, then leaped from my bed. My younger brother peeked from behind his bedroom door, and I beckoned for him to take my hand. We scampered to the top of the stairs. Below us our father—the pack Alpha—shifted to his massive black wolf in a blink of an eye. Our mother raised panicked dove-gray eyes to us.

"Go! Hide!" She urged in Russian before she joined our father in wolf form.

They raced out the door.

I turned to my brother.

"Come, we'll go to the cellar. Don't speak."

He nodded and followed me down the stairs. As I put him ahead of me to enter the cellar, ferocious growls made the hairs on the back of my neck rise. We swung around.

Two giant male wolves stalked towards us. Their jaws snapped. Their intent apparent.

I pushed my brother through the door and slammed it shut yelling for him to lock it. Then I called forth my wolf. I allowed my body to relax and accept my wolf to take over. The sensations of my bones reshaping and muscles lengthening to shift me from my human form to that of my white blonde white wolf blocked out all else. Crackling and a flash found me on all fours within moments. I howled in fury.

The wolves glanced at each other, then launched themselves at me. I jumped aside and spun around to sink my fangs into the hind leg of the one closest to me. He roared.

My only thought was to lead them away from my brother. I had to keep him safe! A glance over my shoulder confirmed they were behind me. I darted out the front door. Then froze.

Surrounded by dozens of unfamiliar wolves, members of my pack in human and in wolf form fought for their lives. Instead of the fresh saltwater of the Gulf of Finland east of the Baltic Sea, the scent of blood, smoke, and stark fear assaulted my nostrils. Screams of anguish and bellows of anger filled my ears. To one side, a ring of fire kept she-wolves separate from the rest. It lit up the inky black night. We were losing to the invaders. My heart sank.

A brutal slash to my flank pulled my gaze from the grisly scene. I yelped in pain and staggered sideways. The pair of wolves swatted me towards the other she-wolves. A ginormous male in human form lifted me from the ground. With ease he tossed me above the flames. Tips of my fur singed as I hurtled through the air before I landed on all fours and rolled.

The wind knocked out of me made me pause.

"Sasha! What are we going to do?"

I glanced up at a she-wolf. Her amber eyes wide with fear. Others gathered around. As the Alpha's daughter, they looked to me for guidance. Despite the aches and scratches, I shifted back to my human form.

The battle slowed as they killed more males and herded the remaining females. Only my mother and father remained standing, now in human form. A male spoke in low tones to them My father cursed and jerked against the three males who held him. The leader nodded his head at a wolf. It leaped onto my mother and ripped out her throat. I screamed. My father's roar silenced as another wolf tore his throat open. I screamed until no sound came out.

A sharp cry brought my attention to our house. A wolf dragged my brother by his arm. Blood poured from the punctured flesh.

"NET!!!"

I shifted and ran through the flames. Fire caught my fur. I rolled to put some of it out, then charged towards my brother. Protect him!

The male yelled for the fire left on my fur to be extinguished. A heavy blanket fell over me. I stumbled to the ground snapping my jaws. A gurgled scream let me know they killed my brother. Beneath the blanket, I thrashed wildly and bit at my captors. A searing pain, then darkness.

I thought nothing could be worse than that night. But I've watched in horror as Kirill and his henchmen drag one she-wolf after the other, clawing and screaming into the breeding barn. Helpless to save them, I prayed to the gods I would get away before I came into season. At twenty-five, it could happen at any time. Several weeks ago, an opportunity to run occurred while Kirill left to complete a sale.

With fewer males on site of the pack lands hidden in the rural area outside of Philadelphia, it was time. I grabbed the bag hidden beneath the floorboards of the bedroom I share with other she-wolves who have yet to come into heat in the main pack house. A quick glance around, and I ran for my life. Unfortunately, I wasn't careful enough with my tracks. They found me less than an hour later.

A furious Kirill strung me up in the barn and beat me with his leather belt as an example. The other she-wolves and the human females they kidnapped and turned against their will stood with abject terror etched on their faces. They flinched and cried with me as each lash cut into my bare back, leaving trails of fire on my flesh. He tossed me into a stall with a warning I could barely hear over the pain-filled roar in my ears. With effort, I shifted into my white blonde wolf and tucked myself into a ball. The powers of my wolf regenerated my torn skin to heal the wounds.

Now, as I tremble before the enraged Alpha, all sorts of torturous punishments race through my mind. I've seen what he's done to others. The belting he gave me was nothing. I bite back a choked sob. Then yelp as Kirill fists my ash blonde waist-length hair and yanks my head back, exposing my vulnerable throat.

My fearful dove gray eyes meet his harsh obsidian orbs. His wolf flashes in their depths. Lips curl back in a sneer to reveal his canines.

"You think because you are a beauty I will not harm you, Sasha? Is that why you continue to test me?" He snarls.

I swallow audibly, too afraid to verbalize a response.

He yanks my hair again, and I gasp as my eyes close against the pain. Hairs pull from their roots. A tear slips past the corner of my scrunched eyelid.

"*Otvet' mne!*" Kirill seethes between clenched teeth in Russian for me to answer him.

"*N—Net...*" I gasp through the torment. "No..."

"No, what?!"

I pant and respond, "N—No, Alpha *Our Lord.*"

He jerks my head to push my face to the filthy straw. Stale urine fills my nostrils. The stench heightened by my wolf senses. But I don't dare to issue a sound.

The crunch of straw beneath his fancy leather shoes indicates he prowls around me in a circle. A predator seeking its prey. Another shudder racks my body. Puffs of dirt lift to my face as I pant. My head snaps back.

Without warning, Kirill drags the blunt edge of a switchblade from my temple to my jaw. I scream as blood gushes from the ragged wound and drips onto my thin cotton dress. He holds the sides apart. Pain like no other burns my face. My wolf howls in agony.

"The salt will prevent the cut from healing properly. The scar will forever remind you not to disobey me again, Sasha Volkov. When your heat comes, I will make you mine," Kirill growls in my ear.

I cringe and scream until I'm hoarse as the flat of his tongue slides along the cut, lapping at the blood.

He rises to his full height of six feet, six inches. He wipes the switchblade on the front of my dress danger- ously close to my nipple. I shrink back. He chuckles darkly.

"Put her in the silver cuffs. Do not allow her to shift into her wolf."

He spins on his heel and leaves the barn.

Searing flames wrap around my wrists, pinned behind my back as I'm jerked to my feet. I stumble and collapse to my knees.

"Get up or else!" One of his henchmen yells at me in Russian.

So tired and broken, I hang my head. A crack to my temple makes me cry out. Despite it all, I scramble to my feet. The male wolf shifter drags me to a stall and pushes me inside. The door slams shut and the lock clicks into place.

"Sasha. Sasha, wake up! Hurry!"

A moan slips from my parted lips as hands fumble with the silver handcuffs and lift me to my feet. I do not know how long I passed out in the stall. But it's quiet and dark.

My face throbs. Fresh tears fill my eyes. I gasp for breath.

"Sasha! Listen to me!"

The urgent whisper pushes through the fog of pain.

I glance up to find Ivan—one of the younger males Kirill added to his henchmen. I flinch.

"It's okay. I'm helping you get out of here. Kirill went too far. You don't deserve to be treated that way. None of you she-wolves or the human females. I'm so sorry I didn't help before. But now, come on!"

A muscular arm grips me around the waist as Ivan helps me from the stall. Outside, he leads me to the woods. We hurry with only light from the half moon to guide our steps. In silence, we rush on until we reach the road.

A black pickup truck with the headlights off appears before us.

I glance at Ivan questioningly. He nods and opens the passenger seat and lifts me onto it. He whispers for me to stay down, then climbs in behind the wheel and drives away. My heart races, but the steady hum of the engine soothes me to sleep.

"Sasha, we're here."

My heavy eyelids open as Ivan shakes me gently. I glance outside the window. We're at a bus station.

"I can't take you any further," Ivan says as he hands a tote bag to me. "There's a change of clothes. Also, some money. Get as far away as you can—"

"What about you? And the others?"

He shakes his head.

"I can't go. It'll be too obvious. Besides, someone has to help. I'll do what I can. But this goes deeper than you realize. Stay to yourself and don't let any other wolf shifters catch you. Don't worry. Know that I'll stay true to my word. Be safe. Now, go!"

Tears well in my eyes. He reaches past me and opens

the passenger door. With a nod, he urges me on. I thank him and step to the pavement. The tears cascade down my cheeks. More salt fills my wound as I watch Ivan drive away until the pickup truck's taillights disappear in the dark.

I make a pledge to the gods I will help the other she-wolves and turned human females. But first, I have to help myself.

Determined, I head towards the doors of the bus station. Inside, I pull my hair over the side of my face and find the restroom. I rush into a stall and change into a t-shirt, sweater, and a pair of jeans. Toilet tissue stuffed into the toes of men's boots fills the space my smaller sock-covered feet can't reach. I fold the bloodied dress into the tote bag to wash later. I'll need all the clothes I can get.

A large roll of bills sits in the interior zipper pocket of the tote bag. I pull some twenties from it and place them in my jeans pocket for the bus ticket. It won't do to flash so much cash around. Ivan must have given me his savings. I close my eyes and send a prayer of thanks for him and for his safety. The gods know Kirill will lose his mind when he finds me gone. Especially since he wants to make me his.

With the vision of him raging around the barn, I hurry to the ticket window. The first bus goes to Washington, D.C. I don't want Kirill to track me on the immediate departures, so I wait for the fourth one—a bus to New York City. It's a big enough place to hide amongst the millions of people. Become invisible, untraceable.

During the ride, I can't sleep. My mind churns with

thoughts of what lies ahead, where will I stay, how will I make money. By the time the sun rises, we pull into Port Authority Bus Terminal. I follow the other stragglers off the bus and through the bustling station.

I stop at a rack of neighborhood maps and take a few. Then I enter a store for two disposable mobile phones, a large bottle of water, and a handful of protein bars. The man behind the cash register eyes me suspiciously. I keep my hair over my face and hurry out the door. I can sense his eyes on my back, and my pace quickens.

My wolf whines, wanting me to shift to help ease our pain. But I can't. First, I have to find a place to stay.

"Excuse me."

I pause and glance to my right. A petite human female in her late twenties with a copper complexion, chestnut brown hair, and sparkling hazel eyes peers up at me.

"Yes?" I ask, trying to disguise my Russian accent.

She smiles and extends her hand. Her thumb and index finger hold up a business card.

"I'm Vera Winslow, a work at a women's shelter on the Lower Eastside. You look like you could use a friend," she says as her smile widens.

Discreetly, I sniff the air. No malice surrounds Vera. I take the proffered card and scan it. Not familiar with the city, I have no idea what the shelter is or of its location. I bring my gaze back to her heart-shaped face.

"Come, let me buy you a cup of coffee or tea, if you prefer. There's a diner around the corner. Don't worry, I mean you no harm."

I study Vera and scent the air again. Nothing about her concerns me. Besides, I can more than handle the human female who stands a good four inches below my five feet, eight inches. She barely reaches my shoulder.

"Thank you," I whisper and walk with her to the exit.

The noise of the busy street hits me. Car horns blare. People talk into their mobiles. A fire engine with its siren blasting races by.

The brisk fall air filled with the smells of exhaust, cologne, and fried eggs from a food truck assail my nostrils. The combination overwhelms my wolf. We're used to the clear air of the pack site, the fetid barn notwithstanding.

I shudder at the horrible memory of earlier and push it aside. Focus, Sasha. Find a place to stay and a job.

Vera holds the door to the diner open for me. Inside, she points to a table. As we settle in the booth, the waitress comes over. Vera orders coffee, and I ask for tea. My stomach growls, and she insists I order some breakfast.

Once the waitress leaves us, Vera smiles at me.

"I won't ask you for your name or any personal information. Instead, I'll tell you about the shelter and how we help women who are new to the city. Sounds good?"

I nod. Encouraged, she goes on.

The more Vera talks, the more I relax. She's passionate about her work with the shelter and with helping others. Again, I only sense goodness from her. She continues to talk while I eat an omelet loaded with bacon, ham, and sausage. My wolf craves the protein to help with our healing. She purrs content with each bite.

Hope blooms in my chest. I thank the gods for putting Vera in my path.

An hour later, we're on a crosstown bus headed for the women's shelter. And a new beginning.

CHAPTER 3

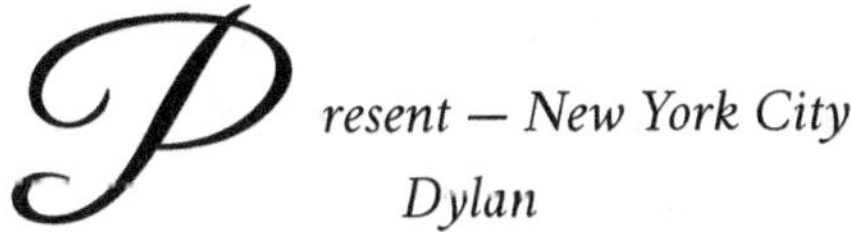

resent — New York City
Dylan

"She said 'no.' Now, leave her alone."

The human male glares at me, pissed I interfered with his hookup attempt. His beady eyes flit over my face, then my body to size me up. A few inches shorter than me, but just as muscular, he sneers.

"Who the fuck asked you for help?"

I lift the beer bottle to my lips and sip slowly. He can get red-faced all he wants as long as he doesn't force the human female. And he damn sure better not put his grubby hands on me.

He snorts at my lack of response and returns his attention to the brunette.

"I bought you a drink. Now, dance with me," he

demands as he grabs her by the elbow and pulls her from the barstool.

Her shocked gasp finishes him.

In a blur of movement, I move her aside and punch him in the mouth. Bone collides with bone as my knuckles crush his front teeth. I ignore the stab of pain and stand over him as he lies on his back, passed out amongst the empty peanut shells and sawdust on the floor. Blood leaks from his slack mouth.

"She said 'no.' Now, leave her alone."

A hush descends on the crowded bar. But only for a moment before the jaded New Yorkers return to their night of drinking and dancing. The bartender calls to me. He smirks and lifts an extra bottle of beer for me.

"Courtesy of the house."

I thank him with a nod as the woman gushes with her thanks. I suggest she call it a night, and she rushes for the door without a backwards glance. Her ass—oh so right lifted by fuck-me heels—captures my attention, but for a moment. I shrug and settle back on my barstool.

The bouncers haul handsy from the floor and drag him out the door.

"Excuse me."

I set the bottle on the bar and glance to my right. A man in his forties, bald, and stocky stands beside me. Another man a few inches shorter than me and built like a linebacker stands behind him. Both dressed in custom-tailored suits to fit their muscular frames. I cock a questioning eyebrow at them.

"The name's Bennett, and he's *The Bull*. It was nice of you to help that woman," the first man says, then pauses for my response. When nothing comes forth, he continues. "You move with power and grace, well controlled, especially for a guy of your size. Do you fight?"

I snort and shake my head.

"What do you think?"

Bennett chuckles and turns to *The Bull*.

"We got a live one here, huh?" He asks, and the other man laughs. If you call a half grunt laughter. Bennett glances back at me. "Listen, I represent fighters at exclusive events for the richest of the rich spectators. The bets earn winners thousands of dollars for a night in the cage. You could rake it in. If you're interested, give me a call."

He holds up a business card.

I scent the air surreptitiously. He's not a liar and doesn't carry the stench of deceit. I take the card and scan it—only Bennett and a 917 mobile number appear in black against a white background. With a nod, I slip it into my jeans pocket and pick up my beer. End of conversation.

Bennett chuckles as he strides to the door.

"Listen. Go in there and take them out one after the other. They'll get more experienced as the night goes on. Your goal is to make it to the end. That's when the headliner enters the cage. Tonight, it's *The Anaconda*. He likes to leap up and lock his thighs around his opponent's neck, drag them to the mat, and squeeze the shit out of them…"

Bennett rambles on with his advice.

It didn't take me long to decide the time in the cage would do me well.

I just arrived back in the United States after four years of traveling the path to enlightenment, as predicted by that barred owl. I sought a return to my Viking roots. Time spent wandering through Scandinavia and Europe provided the separation I needed from the Miami Wolves Pack.

No regret for my actions lingers. Aside from my mother, I don't give a damn about Jagger or any of the others. I've had to put myself first my entire life. And now, I'm a lone wolf.

Despite Jagger's demand I get permission from the Alpha in whose territory I enter, I settle in New York City. I could have gone anywhere, but the city drew me to it. And I rely on my gut instincts. So, if Garrett Moen has a problem with me being here, let him tell me. Otherwise, fuck him too.

I'll use my brawn—and my wolf senses—to win in this underground fight club. Not my past and no one make me weak. And an anaconda can't match a wolf.

I crack my neck as I bounce on the balls of my bare feet. My shoulders and legs shake to loosen up my muscles. There's not much I need to do to prepare for an MMA fight. Years of training ingrain the moves and my wolf's cunning guides me.

A curvy, brown-skinned beauty in the fight club's uniform—a tight tank top and skimpy ass-cheek-bearing shorts—enters the room. She gives me an appreciative up and down. Her gaze moves from the paw print tattoos on my pecs to the bolts of lightning along my arms and the sunburst on my right flank. Its rays stretch across my eight-pack abs. I know her gaze reaches my impressive junk in the black compression shorts when her eyes widen on a gasp.

She winks at me, then tells Bennett it's time for the first round. With a dazzling smile, she wishes me good luck before she sashays ahead of me as my escort to the cage. Her grip-worthy hips call to my wolf, who howls in delight, tongue lolling from the side of his mouth.

Damn. It's been too long since I got laid.

I ignore the catcalls as the spectators cheer for their favorite fighter and duck into the cage. At six feet, seven inches, the doorframe isn't high enough to accommodate an upright entry. But it gives me an eyeful of my escort's round rear. I smirk as my cock twitches inside the protective—and restrictive—cup. When the night ends, I'll have her bouncing on my hungry dick.

My gaze slides to the human male already in the ring. I size him up. His meager muscles let me know this will be a quick twenty-five minutes. An hour and a half later, I face The Anaconda. True to form in the fifth round, he tries his signature move only to be thwarted by my wolf. I duck under him and wrench around to grapple him. Held in a half guard, I keep my weight on his prone body for control and land vicious ground strikes. The constant threat of submission makes it easy for me to maintain control for the last five minutes of the final round.

Some in the crowd hiss as they witness the beating of their favorite fighter while others cheer for me. Above the shouts, I hear Bennett chant *The Beast*. I smirk at his use of the pack's name for me. He'd asked for a name, and I gave it to him, not realizing he'd use it.

The referee calls the end of the match.

I spring to my feet and walk to the side of the cage to await the judges' decision. The three judges combine the points they awarded us for each round to determine the winner. If we tie, then they'll declare the match a draw. I have no doubt I'm the winner. So, I take a swig from the water bottle the trainer passes to me and wait.

The ring announcer enters the cage. He reads the fight judges' scorecard totals and proclaims me the winner bay unanimous count, time of finish, and method. I nod. My wolf saunters. Bennett whoops.

My escort enters the cage and hits me with another dazzling smile. Yeah. She leads me back to the room. I shut the door behind me and pin her to it. She gasps as her back hits the worn wood. But her legs wrap around my hips.

I bend my knees and rest her weight on my thighs while I yank my shorts down and toss the offensive cup to the floor. I fist the base of my thick dick and stroke as it lengthens. Her eyes follow each movement. Her little pink tongue pokes out to moisten her full lower lip.

"You've had your eye on my cock all night, little girl.

You want it or not?" I growl. My wolf claws beneath the surface, hungry to partake of her bountiful feast.

Her mouth opens and closes, then she nods.

"Your words, little girl. I will have your words."

"Y—Yes—" I slam all ten inches inside of her little pussy in one brutal thrust. "Oh, God, YES!"

My hips snap as I piston in and out of her tight, hot cunt. Fuck, she feels so good. My wolf pants in agreement. Ramped up with adrenaline, I use her hard and fast.

Long fingernails dig into my shoulders as she holds on. She cums three times, screaming like a Valkyrie before I seek my release. With a mighty roar, I unleash a torrent of jizz inside of her sopping wet snatch. It triggers another orgasm for her. Brown eyes roll back in her head as her mouth hangs slack.

I lower her to her feet and slip out of her tantalizing heat. A smirk lifts the corners of my mouth as my jizz dribbles to the floor to puddle between her quivering legs. No need to worry about a condom since she's not in heat and a wolf shifter can't get human ailments.

She slumps against me, so I carry her to the chair then go to the bathroom for a warm wet cloth to clean her. While we fucked, Bennett tried to open the door. But I kept it closed with the force of my thrusts. Now, I answer his tentative knock with a demand to hold on. Ladies first and all. Once she's sorted, I open the door.

Bennett scans the room. His nostrils flare at the musky scent of sex in the air. Then grins at me.

"She's a prize. But I've got your winnings for the night.

You tell me what's better," he says as he hands me a wad of rolled-up bills.

I snort.

Little does Bennett realize I'm a billionaire many times over. I don't need the money. I need the release. A way to channel my anger and to calm my wolf.

I may be all brawn with little brain. But I know a smart business decision when presented with one. Years ago, I invested in an environmentally aware oil drilling company in the Gulf of Mexico when it first started based on a tip. I'll never have to worry about being ranked the lowest in a pack ever again—for status or for money. And I take care of my mother foremost.

My sated escort wakens from her blissed-out nap. I peel a few hundreds from the wad and kneel before her. Her eyes widen at the cash and her cheeks flush as she shakes her head vehemently.

"Not a payment, little girl. This is a thank you for bringing me luck on my first fight night. Treat yourself to a spa day. You have a bit of blood on your pretty manicure," I tell her with a quirk to my mouth. The half moons in my shoulders agree.

Her flush deepens as a smile plays at the corners of her lush mouth.

"Okay, thank you, *Beast*," she purrs lustily.

I help her to the door and smile as I close it behind her.

"And a charmer. You'll do well, *Beast*," Bennett says with a chuckle as he passes me on his way to the door. "I'll text the location for the next fight night. You're about to be famous."

After a quick shower, I change into a hoodie, joggers, and unstrung heavy boots. I sling the duffle bag across my chest and head out for a meal. My cock may be satisfied. But my wolf needs protein to help heal me from a night of back-to-back fights.

Sasha

"A burger rare. Fries. And a Coke."

"The meatloaf with mashed potatoes and a coffee."

Silence.

I glance up from my pad to the third human male seated in the booth when he doesn't place his order like his friends. I pull my hair further over the disfiguring scar on my cheek and angle my face away. He didn't notice it. So, I raise an eyebrow as my pencil hovers over the pad.

"Anything for you?"

He licks his thin lips. A gleam dances in his watery blue eyes as he looks me up and down.

I curse the ill-fitting waitress uniform. The too tight white t-shirt with the Lower Eastside twenty-four-hour diner's logo emblazoned in red across my breasts draw his attention like a bullseye. Instead of his eyes on my face, they leer at my chest. *Fu...* Yuck.

"You from Russia, sweetheart?"

I take a deep breath and try again.

"Would you like to order something to eat?"

He braces the vee of his index and middle fingers on either side of his mouth, then flicks his tongue in and out in rapid succession.

"You," he says after the obscene gesture.

"Not on the menu," I snap, then spin on my heel.

"Okay! Okay! I'll have the western omelet and a coffee. Damn. No need to be all sensitive."

I wave in recognition of his order but don't break my stride towards the kitchen. Tammy—the other overnight waitress—offers me a sympathetic smile as I pass her. I roll my eyes in disgust.

It's been a few weeks at the diner. Most of the time, the customers are pleasant. Usually, staff from the hospital nearby or construction workers on the early morning shift. These guys smell of cheap liquor, sweat, and perfume. They must be ending a night of clubbing.

I place the order with the cook and set up a tray for their drinks.

"Oh my God! Get a look at that stunner! Oh shit! He's looking this way!"

The hairs on the back of my neck rise. My wolf moves from the edges of my being, alert and ready to defend me. Her tail sweeps side to side. Cautious eyes peer in the newcomer's direction.

I don't have to lift my gaze from the soda dispenser to

know a wolf shifter entered the diner. All I can do is pray he's not from Kirill's pack. My heart thuds against my ribs at the thought of being dragged back to Pennsylvania to face an enraged Kirill. Sweat pricks under my armpits. A shudder racks my body.

Coke spills onto my trembling hands down to the floor.

Thankful for the distraction, I drop to a squat and take a deep breath. I glance around frantically to gauge my chances of reaching the back door.

"Good morning. What can I get you?" Tammy purrs. "Hey, are you okay, honey? You look pale! Sit down. I'll get you a glass of water."

Suddenly, my wolf leaps for joy. She lands on all fours and rolls over to her back, legs spread, throat and belly bared in submission. Dove gray puppy eyes stare up at me as her tongue lolls to one side. Gone is my fierce protector.

I gasp.

No! It can't be! Now? Here? In the middle of New York City with millions of people around, in the early hours, he appears. I shake my head from the stupor. The force of it jostles my wolf. She sits up and stares at me woebegone.

No!

I jump to my feet and make a run for it. I ignore the male shifter's gruff call to stop and shouts for ketchup from the three guys in the booth. Instead, I flee through the kitchen's swinging doors, past the surprised cook, and out the back door to the side alley. In my haste, I stumble over abandoned crates. But don't stop. Arms and legs pumping like mad, I put as much distance as possible between me and the diner.

I can't let anyone find me, not even my fated mate. The one decided for me by the gods themselves.

CHAPTER 4

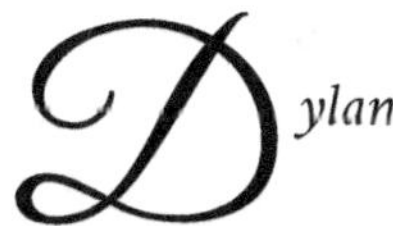ylan

"I DON'T BELIEVE in the whole 'fated mate' story. What? You're born knowing the scent of your fated mate. Then spend years of your life waiting for her to just happen to cross your path. A fated mate who can be anywhere in the world? Nah, dude. Not buying it one bit."

I rolled my golden eyes and huffed as I crossed my bulging biceps across my chest.

The flashback ten years ago when Jagger, Viggo, Tag, Rust, and I were in the Everglades for a multi-pack run in hopes Jagger would find his mate replays. I dismissed his longing for his fated mate instead of any one of the many she-wolves who flung themselves at the prince of the pack.

But one whiff of the unique scent forced my knees to

buckle and drove my wolf wild. Woody and spicy like the forests of Finland when I ran through them in wolf form made my heart race. I don't blame the other waitress. I must have frightened her with the sudden blanching of my normally tanned face. Hell, even my hands shook as I leaned against the counter

My fated mate toppled *The Beast.*

And I didn't even get to talk to the she-wolf. I barely glimpsed her as I staggered to the counter. She ran away as though Garmr—the blood-stained wolf that guards the gates of Hel in Norse mythology—nipped at her heels.

But what I saw made my cock jump to attention.

A curtain of silky, waist-long ash blonde hair trailed behind her. Long, toned legs carried her away. I watched, enchanted by her sleek body. Young and nubile.

Fuuuck!

I roll over in my empty king-size bed and punch the pillow. A growl rumbles from the depths of my chest.

She must have flown like the wind because I gave chase, only to lose her scent. It simply vanished.

When I returned to the diner, the waitress and cook refused to give me her name or her mobile number. They gaped at me when I asked for the information. Then told me I had to leave if I insisted upon getting her details. I stormed out. The door banged on its hinges.

However, it's just as well.

I have no interest in a mate—fated or otherwise. I'm a lone wolf for a reason. No one to tie me down. No one to be accountable to.

No one to disappoint. Like my father did my mother and me.

Some may say I shouldn't let his actions dictate my future. Live my life as I see fit. I disagree.

How I see it is me on my own. Doing what I want when I want to do it. No baggage to tie me down. Period.

The 5 a.m. alarm goes off on my mobile. I hurl it across the room. It clatters against the wall, then drops to the floor and shatters. I won't say like my heart at the loss of my fated mate…

After changing into running gear, I take the private elevator for my penthouse to the lobby. Crisp fall air fills my lungs as I stop on the sidewalk on Central Park South. The aroma of roasted chestnuts, pretzels, and coffee from a street vendor's cart fills my nostrils. Yellow cabs zip by. Other early risers troop to Central Park across the street.

The traffic light changes from red to green, and I jog to disappear amongst the red, gold, and orange tipped trees. My wolf whines to run free. Not now. Too many people around who will notice a giant, black, golden-eyed wolf in their midst.

I chose the building on Billionaires' Row for its proximity to the park. Nearly a thousand acres spread before me where, after midnight, my wolf can roam. So many rarely used spots for us to explore.

I growl at the memory of the real estate agent who scoffed at me when I arrived in a zippered hoodie, sweats, and sneakers for the showing of the $25-million-dollar property. I'd just left the gym and didn't have time to change. The metrosexual human male gazed at me with loathing as he explained the seller required an all-cash offer.

Instead of slashing the expression off his face with my extended claws, I pulled up my investment portfolio and lowered my mobile to his eye level. He blinked and looked again, then backpedaled. I ignored him and stalked towards the elevators. He caught up to me and didn't stop squawking until fifteen minutes later, I matched the seller's price.

When he asked if I had a wife and children, I let a warning growl slip. He sputtered how he was curious since the 8,000-square-foot full-floor penthouse has four bedroom suites. I shook my head and turned to the private elevator. Showing over. Purchase complete.

Sure, I have a guest suite ready for my mother should she wish to visit. But that's the extent of the invite list.

I shake my head and increase my pace to lope along the former bridle path. The sounds of nature call to me. A rustle through fallen leaves as a squirrel buries an acorn. Pigeons coo from their nest above. A hoarse, screaming kee-eeeee-arr draws my attention as a pair of red-tailed hawks call to each other soaring over Fifth Avenue. Of course, I would spot birds that mate for life…

I focus my gaze straight ahead and speed up to a full run. Intent on getting away from thoughts of relationships, I ignore other runners surprised by my burst of speed. Fuck it. I won't shift, but I won't hold back. Pleased, my wolf keeps pace.

We run the full loop of Central Park, south from Fifty-ninth Street up north to One-hundred-tenth Street, Fifth Avenue to Central Park West. I set a grueling pace and make it back to my building in just over ninety minutes.

My body hums as I ride up in my private elevator. As soon as the doors open, I yank my sweat-drenched clothes off and jog to my en suite marble bathroom. Warm water sluices over my body from six wall-mounted jets and an overhead rain shower. Steam fills the glass-enclosed space big enough for four adults.

I let my eyes drift shut.

My hand drags the soapy sponge over my heated skin. It tingles from my neck, across my pecs, along the ridges of my eight-pack, to the feathery trail leading to my engorged cock and heavy balls. I bite the corner of my lower lip to stifle a groan as the vision of a naked ash blonde she-wolf floats behind my eyelids.

Steam obscures her face. The silky curtain sways around her full breasts and dips to her taut belly. The tiny tip of her swollen clit peeks from her bare pussy lips. My mouth waters for a taste as the scent of her arousal teases my nose. I inhale deeply, then drop to my knees to bury my face against her mons.

I lift one toned thigh onto my shoulder and spread her open further with my thumbs. My tongue darts out to lick her from clit to puckered hole. On the return, I prod her slick folds and groan when I'm rewarded with the first gush of her honey.

She cries out above me and tangles her fingers in the

spiked top of my ebony hair. Her fingernails dig into the buzzed sides of my scalp as she cums again with a mewl.

I growl from the bite of erotic pain. But I won't stop eating her out like a starved wolf. The tip of my cock thumps against my navel. Pre-cum leaks from the plum-shaped head. One hand leaves her cunt to fist my turgid length. I stroke it in time with thrusts of my tongue in her pulsating pussy. My groans vibrate along my tongue to drive her to another orgasm.

She doubles over, legs shaking uncontrollably. Her full breasts press into the back of my head as her hands grip my shoulders. Her throaty moan proves my undoing.

While I feast on her pleasure, I jerk my cock ruthlessly. I buck into my hand until my balls draw up and spew my seed against the marble wall of the shower. My jaw hangs slack. I grab her hips and pull her down with me onto the wet floor. She curls in my lap like a full-belly puppy. I bury my face in her silky strands and sigh.

Then my eyes pop open.

Fuck, Dylan!

Get over it.

Not happening! Not now, not ever. Not even with a supposed *fated mate*.

CHAPTER 5

 asha

"WELL, I'm glad you're back, Sasha. For one, the girl from the afternoon shift who covered for you doesn't know what she's doing. And Cook's been leaning on me more to make up for it."

Tammy ends with an eye roll and pursed glossy lips. Cook dings the bell for a ready order. Tammy checks her manicure as she walks back to the kitchen to pick it up.

After the encounter with that wolf shifter, I had to take a couple of nights off. I didn't want to risk seeing him again. And I'm glad since Tammy says he asked for my name and number. *Net!* Thankfully, she says he hasn't been around.

The last thing I need is for him to know anything about

me. I have to keep a low profile. Kirill cannot find me. No one can.

As I go about the mundane task of refilling the salt and pepper shakers, my thoughts turn from my troubles to the she-wolves I left behind. God knows what's happened since Ivan saved me. I pray he's okay, too. If Kirill finds out Ivan helped me, nothing can save the young wolf from the Alpha's fury.

I shudder. Some salt spills on the counter. I take a pinch with fingers on my right hand and toss it over my left shoulder. No need to add any bad luck to an already terrible situation.

My mobile vibrates in my pocket with a text message. Dusting my fingers off, I pluck it out and smile. Vera. Talk about a godsend. If not for her help from my very first minute in New York City, I would be in a far worse state.

Vera secured a bed for me at her women's shelter and helped me to put together a résumé. I was so nervous about going out to the restaurants Vera came with me and sat at tables while I spoke with the managers. She laughed at how she drank so much coffee she was jittery for days.

She even put me in touch with three women who grad-uated from shelter life and rented an apartment together. One of their roommates moved out, and they offered her room to me. Well, more like a closet with a mattress, floor lamp, and milk crates for clothing. But the sixth-floor walk-up apartment is clean and near the diner and the shelter. So, I can still spend time with my new friend Vera.

The only time we had a disagreement was when she

insisted I go to the hospital about the ragged gash on my face. As he promised, the salt prevented my wolf healing from repairing the damage the switchblade inflicted on my cheek. I refused to seek medical attention. How could I? The risk of a doctor learning of my kind outweighs stitches. I'll have to live with the ugly reminder. At the thought, I pull more hair over the side of my face. At least I got away alive.

I just wish I could do something to help the others. They deserve a fresh start too. But it's not like I can go to the police. What would I say? Oh, hi, I'm a wolf shifter who was kidnapped from my home in Russia, drugged, and forced to stay with an evil Alpha and his henchmen in Pennsylvania as a future breeder. I escaped with help. You have to rescue the other she-wolves and human females turned wolf...

Plus, Ivan says the vile organization goes deeper than I realize. How do I know who to trust? For all I know, other wolf shifters are involved. Some of them have to be since they buy the pups without a care where they came from.

I have to think of something.

With a sigh, I reply to Vera's message to confirm we're on for breakfast later. I'll bring food from the diner, and we'll eat in her office at the shelter. Even though I'm exhausted after my overnight shift, I look forward to the mornings we hang out.

At the end of my shift, Cook gives me extra slices of apple pie since he knows it's Vera's favorite. She laughs it off when I tell her he has a crush on her. I smile and add the slices to the bag, then head to the shelter.

I wave at some of the familiar faces as I pass through the sleeping area. On my days off, I volunteer in an effort to give back. It also makes me feel as though I'm helping others even if I can't do anything about the she-wolves and turned humans. I can't just take my good fortune and do nothing in return.

I spot Vera sitting on a bed, deep in conversation with a new girl. Tears stream down her cheeks as she holds herself around the middle and rocks. My heart clenches at her suffering. I pause, torn whether I should approach. Then Vera lifts her face and sees me. A slight shake to her head lets me know it's best to leave them. I nod and hurry to her office.

The sting of tears pricks my eyelids as I drop into a chair. My head hangs as unpleasant memories hit me. From the deaths of my family and pack to the fear of waking on a freighter with crying she-wolves to the fiery burn of the salt on my face. How could I go from an idyllic life to Hell?

I wipe my tear-stained face with the back of my hand. Tears won't change the past. Only action can make a difference. If only I knew what to do!

Time passes before Vera enters her office. Anger makes her hazel eyes flash. She marches to her desk and sits.

"You know, men can be such horrid creatures! I always think the story I'm told by a new resident can't top the last only to hear of another. Dammit!"

She opens the bag as she continues.

"This time, a call to the police won't do. The guy she ran away from is an underground fighter. He doesn't just get his jollies off in the cage. Oh, no. That's not enough. He has to beat her when he comes home!"

Vera takes a forceful bite of a sausage link, which makes me wonder what she'd do to his dick. If it wasn't a messed-up situation, I'd laugh. Instead, I ask her what she wants to do. I'll help anyway I can.

"There's a fight tomorrow night. She gave me a photo of him and two passes. I'm going to go. I have to see him for myself. If I can get close enough, I'll give him a piece of my mind!"

"But that sounds dangerous, Vera! What if he gets mad?" I envision a raging lunatic screaming in her face like Kirill did to me. "Are you sure?"

"Hell, yes!" Vera says as she nods adamantly. "I'll bring my pepper spray."

"Fine. But I'm going with you"—I raise my hand to stop her protest—"You have two passes. Besides, I can't let my bestie face a fighter by herself."

She grins and thanks me.

I tell my wolf to get ready. I won't shift in front of anyone. But I'll use my enhanced strength to take him out!

DYLAN

. . .

"The lineup tonight has some new fighters. Word is a couple are pretty tough and smart. Use their brains and not just their brawn. Watch for…"

Bennett goes on with his usual pre-fight advice. I tune him out and stifle a yawn.

I barely sleep. As soon as I close my eyes, dreams of the ash blonde she-wolf fill my head. Most of them end with us almost fucking. Others have her calling to me as though she needs me to help her. Her hands reach out to me. Our fingers never touch. Then I force myself awake with a frustrated growl. Finnish woods and spices fade from my nose. Fuck!

Tonight's fights will release the tension coursing through my body. I don't give a fuck who's new, smart, or otherwise. They're no match for *The Beast*.

I crack my neck and head for the door. Enough talk. Time for action.

Beverly winks at me when I step into the hallway. My little escort has become a regular post-fight fuck. She knows I'm not into relationships. So, she goes along for the ride—no pun. I smirk at her, and she spins around with an added shake to that glorious ass.

Chants of *The Beast* greet me as I stride towards the cage. I never bother to respond to the crowd. What do I care? Funny enough, the more I ignore them, the louder they shout. Twisted fucks.

My first opponent mean-mugs me. I curl my lip and let a flash of my wolf appear in my golden eyes. The fighter frowns, then shakes his head, unsure of what he witnessed. I chuckle darkly.

The first few fights go as expected. I win.

On my way back to the cage to face the next to the last opponent, I stumble. My head snaps up, and I scent the air, then scan the crowd. It's not possible! How the hell did my fated... I mean that ash blonde she-wolf get in here—an underground fight club event—in an old warehouse? Not possible!

But her unique scent wafts to my nose despite the stench of sweat, blood, and too many colognes.

Then I see her. Unmistakable with her fair hair amongst a crowd of the typical brunette or blonde. Dove gray eyes widen when her gaze swings in my direction, as though drawn to my presence.

My heart stutters in my chest. Within the protective cup, my cock hardens. I have to adjust my junk and will away the erection. My wolf howls in delight. I tell him to back the fuck up, too.

"What's the matter?"

Bennett's question in my ear makes me jolt. I growl with a curved lip. So enraptured by her beauty, I lost the sense of my surroundings. I shake my head to dispel the pull.

"Nothing."

I stalk ahead, determined to ignore my desire to seek her out again. Not happening. However, during the entire fight, my sneak peeks at the beauty. At last, I can replace the faceless female in my dreams with the actual she-wolf. But do I want to?

A roundhouse kick to my flank snaps me back to the cage. I charge the fighter. I make up for my lack of focus for the rest of the fight. The announcer proclaims me the winner. But it was close. I nod at my opponent and leave the cage.

As I rise to my full height, my eyes move of their own will to the stands. The ash blonde she-wolf watches me. A flush of crimson on her alabaster cheek. A curtain of silk covers the other side. She ducks her head, and it falls over her face completely.

Fuck me if my cock doesn't twitch again.

"You gotta focus. What distracted you?"

I glance down to find Bennett peering at me—a scowl on his face. My shoulder lifts in a shrug, then I get a better idea. I jump down the steps and pull him by the upper arm.

"Up in the stands, there's a female with ash blonde hair. Bring her to me."

Bennett jerks back, his frown deepens.

"What the fuck? Do I look like a pimp to you?"

I growl at the implication to the she-wolf.

"She's not a prostitute," I bark through clenched teeth. My wolf snarls.

"Well, do you know her or something?"

"Yeah, something. Be quick. I don't want her to leave before you get to her."

He mumbles under his breath about me being ridiculous and moves through the crowd.

"You ready, now?"

I glance over at Beverly and nod. Then follow her to my room. I tell her I have to talk business, and she leaves. I have twenty minutes before the last fight. Just enough time to figure out my attraction to the female. Unwanted or otherwise, I have to get her out of my system.

~

SASHA

"ONLY ONE FIGHT LEFT. He must be in it…"

Vera's words have no bearing on me.

The male wolf shifter blows my mind—the very one from the diner. At least that's what my wolf's submissive roll indicates. The moment I sensed eyes on me, she dropped to the ground and bared her throat and belly. Tag wagging with happiness.

I just cannot believe my bad luck. Perhaps I didn't toss enough salt…

He watches me intently until the man behind him speaks. It's enough to break the connection.

I sagged back in my seat. My heart thudded in my chest. The urge to leave pressed me. But I couldn't. Vera and I came intending to confront the girl's boyfriend. That's more important than avoiding the male wolf shifter. Determined not to let his presence get to me, my gaze goes everywhere except for the cage.

But I can't help myself! I'm drawn to him.

He moves with the lethal grace of a powerful predator. Solid muscle sculpted to create a god of a male. Chiseled cheekbones, firm jaw covered with a few days' growth of beard. And those eyes. Golden orbs lit from within by the fire of his wolf.

My wolf pants in response.

When the fight ends, I stare at him. The heat in my core travels to my face. His eyes find me, and I drop my head. It won't do to encourage him in any way. But I can't help to peek up, then sigh as he strides away. I tune back in to Vera.

"I have to admit, the fighters are sexy as hell."

"Tell me about it," I grumble and shift in the seat. My pussy drips with my arousal.

A moment later, the man who was with the male wolf shifter approaches the row where Vera and I sit. I frown and pull my hair over my face. Please don't let him come to us. Unfortunately, the gods deny my prayer. He stops at the end of the row and beckons to me. I point at myself, and he nods.

"Do you know him?" Vera asks, surprised by the man's request to speak with me. She glances between us. "Maybe he knows the guy. You should see what he wants. Come on."

With that in mind, I make my way past the other spectators. Feisty Vera follows.

"Excuse me. I'm Bennett, and I represent *The Beast*. He asks you to join him in his room before his last fight. I'll take you to him," the man says as he leans down to my ear.

Who the hell does he think he is to summon me?! His request may affront me, but my wolf leaps in the air.

Vera tugs on my arm, and I tell her. She reminds me it will get us closer to the fighters to go to their private area. So, I agree. Albeit reluctantly.

The man leads us through the crowd, past the security guards at the entrance to the sectioned-off area, and to *The Beast*'s room door. The man knocks and enters.

The potent scent of the male wolf shifter fills my nose. Pheromones mixed with fresh sweat, smoke from a campfire, and exotic spices. Pure masculinity. My wolf pants.

We lock eyes. His flare with lust and a flash of his wolf. Now, I want to drop to the ground in submission. But I shake my head to clear the thought. Then clear my throat.

"Why did you summon me?" I ask, my voice throatier than it should be. Damn hormones.

A smirk plays at the corner of his full lips.

"You ran away."

I raise an eyebrow when he doesn't continue. I try to remain aloof, but the attraction buzzes around us.

"Yes, well, no matter. What do you want?" I ask as I fold my arms over my chest to shield myself from his piercing stare.

"Uh, excuse me."

Vera steps between us with her mobile held up for him to see the screen.

"Do you know this fighter?"

The golden eyes slide from my face to the mobile. He shakes his head, and glances at Bennett, who steps forward.

"Yeah, he's a new guy, and your next opponent. Has a nasty temper from what I hear," Bennett says with a scowl. "What do you want with the likes of him?"

Vera tells them about the new girl. The more she talks, the angrier *The Beast* gets. I can feel it radiating off him in waves. His fists clench at his sides while a vein on his temple pulsates.

"Don't worry. I'll handle him," *The Beast* growls. He looks pointedly at me and adds, "Wait here. Do not run away again."

I can only nod, titillated by his commanding tone. More arousal soaks the gusset of my panties. A tremble runs through me as his nostrils flare at the scent of my arousal, easily detected by his wolf senses. He pins me with an intense stare and stalks out the door.

"All righty then. Talk about a hunk," Vera says as she fans herself. Then she winks at me. "Seems like you have an admirer, Sasha. Now, how did that happen?"

I groan and cover my face. It feels so hot. I'm embarrassed he could see—and smell—how much he gets to me. Dammit!

"Okay. But seriously, I'm glad he's going to help us. I just wish we could watch the fight," Vera says with a pout.

Who says he's the boss of me?

"Come on, let's go watch!"

We hurry giggling conspiratorially. Then gasp when we see *The Beast* pummeling the guy pinned beneath him on the mat. His hands blur with speed. The impact of the blows rings loud in my sensitive ears. Above the roar of the crowd, I hear the guy's faint cries of promises to not hit a woman ever again.

Vera whoops with her fists in the air. She adds her chants of *The Beast* to the other raucous shouts. I join in happy to see a bully pay for mistreating another person, especially an innocent female.

If only it were Kirill and his cronies defeated so easily.

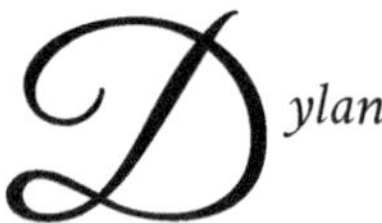

ylan

"GOOD EVENING, Mr. Vang. Would you like me to hail a taxi for you?"

I nod in response to my doorman, and he hustles to the curb, whistle blowing, and arm raised. A cab pulls up. He opens the door. I slip a hundred-dollar bill into his gloved hand as I slide onto the seat. He tips his hat in thanks.

I give the driver the address for the ash blonde she-wolf's diner and settle back against the seat. My thoughts drift to the other night. My cock hardens at the memory of the beauty and how her body reacted to mine. So ripe and ready for me to plunder.

My eyes close as a desperate groan slips past my lips.

Now that I've been so close to scent her arousal and to

see the flush of her face, I can't get her out of my mind. No longer limited to my erotic dreams, she invades my every waking moment. It's driving me wild. My wolf growls in agreement.

I swipe a hand over my face and glance out the window.

The ride from Central Park South to the Lower Eastside will take some time, even after midnight. New York City never sleeps. Just like me, I suppose.

By the time the cab pulls up in front of the diner, I'm salivating for a taste of her honey. If the tantalizing aroma of her arousal is enough to go by, she's sinfully sweet.

I pay the driver plus a generous tip and climb out of the cab. I've put off coming here in hopes the desire would lessen. But the denial only serves to increase the ache. My wolf cocks his head as a trace of her scent lingers outside the door of the diner. She's here.

The bell overhead dings when I push the door open. The waitress from the last time turns towards the sound. She scowls when she recognizes me and steps into the kitchen. A moment later, the ash blonde she-wolf emerges.

Her dove gray eyes full of caution watch as I approach the counter where she stands. She looks poised for flight. Instinctively, I rumble deep in my chest to soothe her. She blinks as her soft lips part on a stuttered breath.

Unexpectedly, her reaction pleases me. The connection fated mates share allows the male to calm his female with the rumble. As much as I want to deny the pull between us, it only gets harder. I stop at the counter.

"Hello."

"Uh, hi. What are you doing here?"

I tip my chin down and gaze up at her through my eyelashes. Her beauty makes me breathless. I take a moment before I respond. She watches me in silence. Except I hear the racing of her heart.

"You left. Again."

She swallows at my gruff accusation. Her cheek reddens.

I want to reach out and pull the silky curtain from the other side of her stunning face. I want to see all of her. The desire proves so strong, my hand reaches up involuntarily. Then it drops quickly when she flinches away from my touch. I frown.

"Yes, I did. You can't make me do anything I don't want to do," she says, a defiant lift to her chin, even as her eyes flit everywhere but my face.

I cock an eyebrow. She continues.

"But I do want to thank you for helping Vera and me. That guy did horrible things to his ex-girlfriend. No one deserves to be abused."

Her voice trails off, and her eyes drop as though she spoke too much. Or perhaps too close to her own experience.

The thought of someone harming her makes me growl. I'd kill the fucker with my bare hands or let my wolf devour his heart. My fists clench on the counter as my eyes flash.

She gasps and stares at me wide-eyed. She swallows audibly and steps back.

Fuck! I scared her. I lower my hands to my sides and control the rage burning within me.

"You're welcome. I do not believe a female should ever come to harm. You know we protect our own," I tell her in a murmur. No need for the other diners to overhear me referring to wolf shifters.

When tears shine in her eyes, my wolf whines.

"Hey, miss! I need some service over here."

A growl rips from my mouth as I spin around to glare at the human male who dares to interrupt us. A soft hand on my arm makes me turn back. My wolf settles on his haunches, feathery tail flicks idly. I'm shocked by how her slight touch calms him instantly.

"I'll be right there," she calls to the male, although her eyes stay on mine. She lowers her voice. "Give me a minute. Why don't you sit in the back booth? I'll come to you when I can."

I nod dumbly and watch as she rounds the counter, pulling her pad from her pocket. She also pulls more hair over the side of her face. It makes me wonder what she's hiding. But for the life of me, I can't imagine what it could be.

I trail behind her and give the male a look of death on my way to the booth. He blinks and gapes like a fish out of water. I curl my lip to reveal a sharp fang and allow my wolf to breach the surface. The male jumps up and bolts for the door.

The ash blonde she-wolf calls after him. But he never stops. She turns to me with narrowed eyes.

"What did you do?" She whisper yells.

I shrug as I respond, "Looks like you have free time now." Then head to the booth.

She follows and sits opposite to me.

"Who hurt you?"

Her alabaster skin blanches as her hand goes to her hair. When I narrow my eyes, she yanks her hand away and stands.

"I—I have to get to work. Please don't come back."

She spins on her heel and rushes to the kitchen. Again.

I use all my control to not run after her and move the hair from her face. All sorts of things run through my mind. But if I act now, I'll wreck this place and frighten her further. I have to proceed with caution. Give her time to get to know me. Open up and tell me what happened. I can help her. And fuck all if I don't want to make her world right.

~

Sasha

"He's here again. Sitting in the back booth as usual. Are you sure you don't want Cook to make him leave? He's a big guy. But Cook will stand up for you. And to think I flirted with the guy the first night he was here. Thank God the stalker didn't latch on to me!"

Tammy pats my arm sympathetically, then goes to help her customer.

I don't need to look up to know *The Beast*—rather, Dylan Vang—has his eyes on me. I can sense his intense stare. He's come to the diner almost every night for the past week. The second time, he wrote his name on a napkin and handed it to me when I passed what I now think of as his booth. He included his mobile number with the words, *Call me anytime you need help.*

Tears blurred my vision, and I rushed away. But I programmed his number into my mobile. Just in case.

Every time I see Dylan, I want to trust him. Tell him about Kirill and the horrible things he does. But how can one wolf shifter—no matter how strong—defeat an entire gang of criminals? Especially one as ruthless as Kirill and his henchmen. Not to mention the entire network. We do not know who's involved.

Plus, I can't put Dylan in a position where he'd get killed, or worse. I'd never be able to live with myself. Despite my denial of us being fated mates, we're connected. What happens to him, I feel, and vice versa. Fortunately, his fights don't bother me since he chooses to participate, or it would destroy me. He can survive the harsh blows, but I cannot. I've had enough of them to know I can't take anymore.

I put in an order for a rare steak and scrambled eggs, then grab a bottle of spring water.

Dylan watches me as I approach his booth. His golden eyes don't miss a move.

"Hi," I say as I hand the bottle to him and slide into the booth. "Your order will be ready in a minute. No fight tonight?"

He takes a sip of the water, and I watch mesmerized as his full lips circle around the rim. The tip of his tongue pokes out as he swallows. The muscles in his throat ripple as the water goes down.

My nipples harden to pebbles beneath the too tight white t-shirt. If he glances down, he'll see how my body responds to his so easily. I press my thighs together to ease the ache gathered in my throbbing pussy. My wolf whines for his attention.

"No. Tomorrow night. Do you want to come?"

My gaze skips to his. I'd like to come, but not in the way he's asking.

As though reading my carnal thoughts, Dylan smirks. He opens his mouth to speak, but the order bell dings.

Thank the gods!

I jump up and hurry to the window. His wicked chuckle follows me. Tammy arches a perfect eyebrow at me. I know my face must be red since it burns, and I'm breathless. That male wolf shifter gets to me like no other! I shake my head at her and pick up the plate.

"Here you go," I say as I place it in front of him. Then gasp when his fingertips brush my hand as he reaches for his fork. Lightning zaps me and courses through my body, setting it aflame with unbridled desire.

"There's no one in your section. Won't you sit with

me?" His already rich baritone voice deepens. It envelops me and makes my body hum.

Before my knees give out, I sit.

He takes a few bites. The way his lips wrap around the fork makes my clit pulse. What scandalous things can they do to it? I shudder as I bite back a moan.

"Tell the little spitfire to come with you."

I blink in confusion, so distracted by my lust-filled thoughts.

"To the fight," Dylan adds for clarification.

Not a bad idea. Vera's mentioned the fight night a few times, angling to get passes from *The Beast*. But I always change the subject.

"I'll ask her. If she agrees, we'll come."

The corner of his mouth twitches, and his eyes sparkle devilishly.

I jump up and tell him I'll send a text message with my answer later. Once again, his wicked chuckle licks at me as I rush to the kitchen.

But no matter the allure of our connection, I will not give in to us being fated mates.

CHAPTER 7

 asha

"You know, a girl could get addicted to these fight nights. All this male testosterone pheromones, sexy-as-sin-erones! Lord have mercy!"

Vera exclaims as she sits on the edge of her seat.

I can't say that I blame her. Their strength—combined with agility—makes them attractive to horny females. And that includes me since I can't stop dreaming about Dylan.

At first, I didn't realize the male wolf shifter was my fantasy lover. Whenever the male appeared in my dreams, shadows shrouded him. No distinct features for me to recognize as someone familiar. I only knew the carnal pleasures he evoked from my more-than-willing body made me cry out loud. Many times, it woke me up. Head thrown back in sheer ecstasy. My body rigid with my core pulsating from a toe-curling orgasm.

Even now, I shift in the seat as my thighs press together to ease the constant ache in my pussy.

The most recent dream revealed Dylan as the mystery male. As before, I'm lying on my bed—naked. Knees splayed. One hand cups my heavy breast, tugging at the peaked nipple. Fingers on the other hand trail down my belly to part my swollen folds, already slick with my arousal. A gasp falls from my slack mouth as my thumb and index finger pinch my sensitive clit. Shadows roll in through my bedroom balcony's open French doors. My heartbeat quickens in anticipation of my fantasy lover's arrival.

But this time, a massive black wolf bursts through the shadows. His golden eyes focus on me to pierce my very soul. For a moment, I'm trapped by his hungry stare. Unable to break the connection. He prowls towards me, head low like a predator stalking its prey.

My mouth opens. But instead of a gasp, a purr slips out.

I blink and gaze down at my hand. White blonde fur covers a paw. My wolf took over!

Without hesitation, I leap from the bed to land grace-fully in front of the male wolf. Pheromones mixed with fresh sweat, smoke from a campfire, and exotic spices fill my nostrils. My body shudders.

He stalks around me. A constant rumble in his chest. He nuzzles my neck, flank, base of tail. With a growl, he rises onto his hind legs and wraps his front legs around my—

"Sasha… Hellooo."

Vera waving her hand in front of my face jolts me from my erotic memories. She huffs and shakes her head.

"You're not even listening to me."

"Oh! Sorry! I got distracted. What did you say?" I ask as my cheeks heat. I do not know how long I spaced out thinking about Dylan. But my body is more aroused than ever. The need is so great. Dammit!

"Well, judging by your dilated pupils, damp forehead, and rosy cheeks, it was a wonderful *distraction*," Vera says with a giggle. "Did it involve your fighter boy?"

I cover my flaming face with my hands.

Vera laughs until she snorts, and I join it.

Can I be any more transparent? Gah!

"And now for the final fight of the night. The one you've all been waiting for… *The Iceman* versus the unde-feated… *The Beast*!"

Vera and I jump to our feet as the crowd roars. We add our voices to chants of *The Beast*. Then hiss and boo when *The Iceman* strides towards the cage. A few minutes later, Dylan stalks out. The crowd goes wild. Wolf whistles and stomping feet fill the old warehouse. It's so loud the blacked-out windows rattle in their casements. The shouts rise to the rafters.

Dylan appears unfazed by the uproar. He stops in the doorway. His golden eyes scan the crowd, then flare with feral lust when his gaze locks with mine. An erotic frisson passes between us. It's so powerful, I gasp as my knees turn to jelly. I grip the metal railing in front of me to steady myself. Desire rages through my body like white-hot lightning.

I don't know if it's my dreams or Dylan's enticing presence, but I ache for the male wolf shifter's touch.

Slowly, he nods his head, never breaking eye contact. Then he steps towards the cage. Before he enters, he turns to pin me with his heated gaze. I shiver. With a satisfied smirk on his handsome face, he pivots and ducks inside.

I barely notice when Bennett appears beside me and sits in the empty seat. He offers a greeting. I nod, too engrossed in the scene below to verbalize an answer.

Over the next half hour, my lust for Dylan reaches a peak. Sweat highlights his sculpted muscles and tattoos. They ripple with each jab and kick. Bulging biceps. Thick thighs. He's the epitome of virility. And my wolf is all for it. To be honest, so am I.

"Ooo wee, chile! That was beyond entertaining. But I have to go. There's an early meeting in the morning," Vera says as she rises from her seat. "You want to share a cab with me? Or do you have other plans?"

She waggles her eyebrows and giggles.

"Whatever! I'm ready. Let's go—"

"Sorry. No can do. *The Beast*—"

"Let me guess… He requests her attendance?" Vera asks, grinning. She hugs me and scoots down the row.

"Hold on there, missy! I'll get a cab for you after I deliver her to him," Bennett says. "He doesn't want you leaving unescorted."

Vera's eyebrows raise impressed by Dylan's chivalry. My heart soars since he cares about my bestie's safety.

"Okay," we say in unison, then giggle.

As I follow Bennett to Dylan's room, my heart goes from soaring to beating frantically. What will happen once we're alone? My wolf sways her tail. Oh gods!

~

DYLAN

As I leave the cage, I watch Bennett leading the ash blonde she-wolf and her friend from the stands. Good.

My cock comes to life in the protective cup. Too bad I still don't know what name to call when I jerk off to her vision. I don't know how much longer I can hold off from fucking her like the feral beast I am.

I follow the new escort to my room. My wolf wouldn't let me interact with Beverly once the she-wolf made her appearance. He became more boisterous than usual. However, this time I fully agree with him. I have no interest in any other female.

The escort leaves me at the door, and I enter. Quickly, I pull the compression shorts off and throw the restrictive cup to the ground. I sigh in relief and stroke my aching cock as I stride to the make-shift shower.

Even over the water's spray, I hear the room door open, and the she-wolf tell her friend good night. She giggles and tells her to get her groove on. The she-wolf laughs throatily, and my cock thumps against my high-pack abs.

So, she's as keyed up as I am. Time to do something about it. Dreams don't cut it...

I wait for the door to shut and listen as she moves about the room. I turn off the water and wrap a towel around my hips. My cock refuses to go down. It tents the front of the towel. I shrug. She might as well see what she's about to get.

Her jaw drops when I step into the room. Dove gray eyes darken to obsidian as she gapes at me from head to cock—where they linger—and toe. I watch, pleased, as her nipples pucker beneath her thin blouse. Long, lithe legs encased in fitted jeans rub together.

I growl and stalk towards her.

"Oh, no, Little Wolf. I give you pleasure."

She gasps and backs up until her ass bumps into the wall.

My forearms on either side of her head cage her in. I bend my knees and press our thighs together. My nose drops to the side of her throat where I nuzzle the soft skin.

She shivers as her warm breath pants against my wet hair.

"D—Dylan, what—"

"Hush. Only tell me your name."

She hesitates, and I rumble in my chest. With a sigh, she says, "Sasha... Sasha Volkov."

"*Saaashaaa,*" I breathe as I trace open-mouthed kisses along her slender neck and press my cock against her jeans-covered mons. The tip slips from beneath the towel. Pre-cum dribbles down the side. I groan at the friction. "*My* Sasha."

"*O, bogi…*"

I press more kisses to her heated flesh and grind my groin. But it's not enough My wolf whines in agreement, pacing on the fringes, wanting to come forward. To claim our fated mate.

A frustrated growl blows warm air against her neck. She shivers. I push the thought of claiming her to the far corners of my mind. Right now, I want to savor her.

I drop to my knees and tug the button at her waist. Her hands grapple with mine. I raise my eyes to her face.

"Let me taste you, Sasha. I need your honey on my tongue. Now."

She blinks as her mouth works around a soundless response. I return to my task and rip her fly open. The button and zipper pieces scatter. She squeaks. Her palms slap against the wall as her hips move forward.

I yank the jeans past her knees and lift her up to tuck my head between her quivering thighs. A flick of my wrist and the damp thong drops to the floor. I bury my face in her slick pussy and inhale her musky arousal. We groan as one when my tongue plunges between her swollen folds.

Her hips undulate as I lap at her sweet honey. Determined to make her cum, I brush my nose against her sensitive clit with each lick. Her fingers grip my hair as her pussy walls constrict. I plunge two thick fingers beneath my tongue. She's so tight.

"D—D—DYLAN!"

Sasha screams my name as her cunt gushes for me. I growl and swallow every single drop, forcing two more orgasms from her. She writhes through the aftershocks as I lick her clean. Her intoxicating flavor is fresh on my tongue.

Just as in my dream, my fist jerks my turgid length. I surge into my hand until my balls draw up and jettison my seed against the wall. I groan in relief. But it's still not enough. More! My wolf demands. I agree.

I kiss her pussy lips and slip her legs over my head before I tower over her. Her head hangs. The silky curtain of her ash blonde hair covers her beautiful face. I hold her chin between my thumb and forefinger to tilt her head up.

The air leaves my lungs.

A wide, jagged scar runs from her temple to her jaw. The raised red mark emphasized by the surrounding alabaster skin. Her wolf healing did little to repair the damage to her otherwise unblemished face.

She sighs content and opens her eyes. One glimpse of my stormy expression, and she yanks her face away and covers the side with her hair.

"Who the fuck did this to you?" I thunder.

She startles and shakes her head.

"Don't... Please. I—I have to go," she whispers and clutches at her torn jeans. She attempts to step around me, but I block her path.

"No! You will tell me what happened and tell me now, Sasha," I command.

Our connection as fated mates will not allow her to ignore my demand. But she must not realize it because she gapes at me before she speaks. Tears spill from her eyes as she recounts the horrors of her kidnapping to the cutting and her escape.

The entire time, I pace the room uncaring I'm naked. I punch holes into the walls a few times. Kick the table and throw the chair. Only pieces of wood litter the floor. By the time she's finished, the room resembles a disaster zone.

"Where. Are. They." I bark.

Sasha flinches, and I scrub my hand over my face. I stride over to her and bend my knees to bring our eyes on level. She lowers her chin to cover her face. I brush the strands behind her back.

"Baby, I don't mean to frighten you and do not hide your face from me," I say as I rub her arms. "You are beautiful, and I want to see all of you."

Her lower lip trembles as more tears fall.

With a groan, I cover her mouth with mine. I push my tongue past her parted lips and coax her tongue to tangle with mine. A shock runs through me when our tongues entwine. She must feel it too because she moans and wraps her arms around my neck.

I stand up, lifting her from her feet to hold her flush against me. My cock presses into her belly. She winds her legs around my hips.

"*Saaashaaa*... My Sasha. You undo me," I groan against her kiss-swollen lips.

I want to fuck her so badly. But not here. I put her down and catch her by the elbows when she teeters.

"Let me get dressed, and we'll leave," I say, my voice gruff with unexpected emotion.

She nods and fusses with her jeans. I pull the cord from my hoodie out and tuck it in the loops of her jeans, then tie it tight. She smiles at me. Fucking gorgeous. My beauty.

I tear myself away from her, scoop up her thong, and dress quickly. With my duffle slung across my side, I take her hand and lift her onto the seat of my Harley-Davidson, then guide it towards the door.

Most of the people left, so I maneuver us past the stragglers and out the main doors. I lift her off the motorcycle and hop on. I hold my hand out to help her mount up behind me.

"Sorry, I don't have a helmet. But you'll be safe," I say, then shift on the seat to stare into her eyes directly. "You will always be safe with me, Sasha Volkov."

She bites her lower lip and nods. I return the nod and reach back and pull her arms tight around my waist.

"Hold on. Move with me. Do you understand?"

"Yes, Dylan."

I start up the Harley, and we zip away.

CHAPTER 8

asha

I TRY NOT to think about what could happen if I tell Dylan Kirill's name and the location of the pack. So instead, I relive his erotic kisses.

He played my body like a fine violin. His tongue mimics the taut bow as it strummed over my pussy. The way he was so forceful and demanding makes me bite back a moan.

My core pulses, and I tighten my hold around his waist. I keep my cheek pressed against his firm back. The muscles flex with each movement as he steers the motorcycle. Being this close to him with my inner thighs pressed to his hips and legs makes my core clench.

The gods help me, but I want more of Dylan Vang.

"I smell fresh honey, *Saaashaaa.*"

I squeal with embarrassment and bury my face in his hoodie as we wait for the traffic light to change. Thankfully, it doesn't take long. Dylan chuckles wickedly and surges ahead.

I'm glad he's not as angry as before. I know Dylan won't ever hurt me. But he was ferocious. His wolf barely contained. I felt sorrier for the room than having any fear of him.

And what will happen when we get to wherever he's taking me?

I don't want to ask, just go with the flow. Let him take control. It's been so long since I've had to do everything for myself. I'm happy for the chance to let him take over. Does that mean we'll follow the decision of the gods we're fated mates? I can't say. But if what we just shared hints at what we could be together, I'm not mad.

We pull into an underground garage, and Dylan stops the motorcycle in a space marked Reserved PH. I notice a Range Rover and another fancy motorcycle sit in two other spaces with the same sign. The fourth space remains empty.

"I don't mind you holding me. But we're here."

I giggle and slip off the bike. Dylan smirks and hops off. He takes my hand and leads me to an elevator where he places his palm on a plaque. The doors slide open, and we step inside. Another palm placement and the elevator rises. Only one button on the panel, and it too bears the PH mark.

He's silent as we ride up. Surreptitiously, I glance at him in the reflection of the elevator doors. He's almost a foot taller than me, so I peek from beneath the long fringe of my eyelashes. His eyes stare straight ahead, rarely blinking. The set of his jaw is rigid, as though he's holding back. His broad chest expands on a deep inhale. Then he pins me with his golden gaze.

I bite my lower lip and flick my eyes away.

"I sense you watching me, Little Wolf."

I blow a breath and tilt my head up to look at him. He cocks an eyebrow.

"I don't want you to worry about me, Dy—"

His growl makes me stop. His eyes flash with his wolf.

The elevator doors open with a ping.

Relief washes over me as he lifts his arm and motions for me to step out ahead of him. We enter a foyer where double wooden doors with two consoles topped by flower-filled vases flank the entrance. Once again, Dylan places his palm on a plaque. The lock disengages, and he pushes the doors open.

I step past him and freeze.

Central Park stretches out in front of me. From the southern end to the north, it's lit by streetlamps along its paths. The ponds and lakes glitter. With my enhanced vision, I can see the glorious colors of the fall leaves. It's absolutely breathtaking.

"If it were a few hours earlier, we could have run as wolves through the park. I do it several times a week. It's the main reason I bought this place."

And by this place, Dylan means the most luxurious home I've ever seen. Central Park is so visible because a wall of floor-to-ceiling windows allows its expanse to reach right inside the home, straight into the living room.

The outdoor view is spectacular. But the interior rivals it. Its modern decor has a monochromatic color palette of grays—from light like my eyes to charcoal. Natural wooden tables complement the clean lines of the sofas and chairs with plush throws. The natural light from the moon sweeps inside. The minimalism isn't harsh. It makes the space more livable.

I could see myself curled up on the sofa, reading a book or gazing out the window. So comfy.

"So comfy? I'm glad you like it," Dylan says.

I blush, not realizing I spoke aloud, and walk across the wooden floors towards the windows. The heels of my booties click on the polished surface. I sense Dylan close behind me and add an extra sway to my hips.

"Careful, Little Wolf," he warns with a low growl.

My nipples pucker while my pussy drips.

"Mmm… Delicious."

When we reach the wall of windows, Dylan lifts my palms to the glass.

"Do not move," he murmurs in my ear as he unties the hoodie cord at my waist.

Dylan crouches behind me and removes my booties, then tugs my jeans off. His hands grip my hips and angles them back as he rises. He kicks my feet apart until they're at the distance he wants.

I'm almost bent in half with my face close to the glass between my palms. My warm pants fog the window. I detect the faint whisper of his joggers dropping to the floor moments before he slams his ginormous cock inside my pussy.

I scream.

He groans.

"Fuck. Me. So tight, *Saaashaaa*. Fuuuck!"

His grip tightens on my hips. He drags his dick back, and my pussy tries to suck him back inside.

"So greedy for my cock, Little Wolf. Look at how you gobble me up. Fuck… So beautiful."

I whine from the stretch and burn of his big dick. But I want some more. I wiggle my hips and push back against him, trying to impale myself on his cock. He spanks both butt cheeks and growls.

"I told you before, *I* give you pleasure, Little Wolf! You do not take it."

He spanks my ass a few more times, and my pussy gushes. He growls and plunges back in.

I scream again. My legs quiver as I rise on tiptoe.

Dylan pauses and drags his cock out to the tip. The scent of fresh blood floats in the air. He sucks in a breath.

"Are you a *virgin*, Little Wolf?" He asks in a raspy voice.

I bite my lower lip and lower my head. I don't want him to stop. Not treat me any differently. I refuse to answer.

Two sharp cracks to my ass have me speaking up.

"Y—Y—Yes!" I shout as I peer at him over my shoulder.

His golden eyes glow before he throws his head back

and howls. The feral cry sends a shiver down my spine. He lowers his gaze to meet mine, and I can see his wolf clearly.

"MINE!" He roars.

My cheek nearly hits the window as his cock slams deep into my pussy. I slap my palms on the glass and brace myself for the mounting he's about to give me. My juices drip down my inner thighs and pool between my feet.

The sounds of Dylan's feral growls and grunts mingle with my cries of wild abandon. Flesh smacks against flesh and reverberates around the living room. The carnal scent of our fucking fills the air. It's addictive. I can't get enough of Dylan. I growl in frustration.

Once my body acclimates to his size and catches his grueling rhythm, I meet him thrust for thrust. Dylan growls his approval and slides his hand around my hip to tweak my sensitive clit. I throw my head back and howl as an orgasm overtakes me.

Sweat coats my fevered skin. My slippery palms slide along the glass, leaving trails of moisture in their wake. Another orgasm rips through me, and my toes curl. I thrash my head from side to side.

"*O, bogi…*" I scream to the gods.

Dylan takes me with feral dominance and desire. Not once do his brutal strokes slow. In fact, his pace increases until I can barely keep up with him. He grunts and digs his fingers into my hips. My feet leave the floor. He bends his knees and pumps up into my elevated pussy.

I reach back and grip his forearm while my other palm presses on the window for balance.

The angle causes a delicious burn. My pussy clamps on his cock like a vise. He howls and pumps faster. My butt smacks against his groin again and again.

Dylan lowers me, and I wobble on my feet. His tight grip prevents me from collapsing to the floor in a puddle

My breath quickens when his already ginormous cock grows thicker. I clamp down on him again, and he howls.

One arm bands around my waist while the other hand sweeps my long hair to the side. It hangs over my shoulder, nearly reaching the floor. His chest presses against my back and his hand wraps around the front of my throat. I can't move.

His hot breath blows across the sweaty skin at the juncture where my neck meets my shoulder. Warm liquid drips on the spot. Then pain sears me at the same time as the base of his cock expands and locks at the entrance of my core. The swell of his cock excruciating. Blood trickles down my shoulder. Liquid heat explodes in my pussy. I howl and struggle to break free of his hold.

Dylan's hand and arm tighten like bands of steel as his extended canines sink into my flesh. His mouth opens, then clamps back on the same spot. The serum from his canines lodges his scent under my skin to mark me as his permanently. He shakes his head to deepen the claiming bite.

"MINE!" He growls against my skin as he licks the spot.

My legs give out.

I didn't expect for this to happen.

DYLAN

I sit on the sofa and watch Sasha as she sleeps in my king-size bed. She's curled in a ball on her side. Her silky hair fans out on the pillow and down her back. She looks so small and vulnerable. I ache to go to her and pull her into my arms.

But Sasha hasn't uttered a word since I issued my claiming bite over an hour ago. Even while I held her on my lap until my knot deflated. She remained silent the entire time I bathed her in the shower, dried her body and hair, and put one of my t-shirts over her head. I carried her to the bed and tucked her beneath the silk sheets. She rolled to her side and closed her eyes.

I pressed a kiss to her soft lips, then to my claiming mark and murmured for her to rest.

Fuck!

I can't even blame it on my wolf. I did it. And willingly.

The feel of her untouched cunt wrapped around my cock combined with her tantalizing, unique scent, and the way she responded to me made me a goner. I had to claim my fated mate. No more denial.

My canines extended and released the serum bearing my scent to mark her permanently. Going on pure instinct, I gripped her close and bit.

Simultaneously, the knot at the base of my cock I

usually suppress swelled to lock me inside of her tight pussy. The overwhelming urge to fill her womb with my seed triggered the expansion. Make her belly round with my pup. Claim her in every way.

Sasha Volkov is mine. Forever.

She may be upset I did it without discussing it with her. But she knows the ways of our kind. She's the daughter of an Alpha. Plus, there's no denying her desire for me, either. She submits to me. Her reactions to my growl and my rumble are beyond question. She knew she was mine the moment I walked into that diner. The fact she ran away makes no difference.

Hell, I was running away from *her* call. Then I succumbed.

So, she claimed me as much as I claimed her. She bears my mark on her neck. I wear hers on my heart. Both indelible.

"NET!!!"

Her cry rouses me from my musings. Her fists fly through the air, undoubtedly assailing her attackers.

I jump to my feet and rush to comfort her. I pull my fated mate into my arms and caress her back as I rumble deep in my chest to soothe her.

Tiny fists strike my solid chest as her screams of *No* increase in volume. Only when I intensify my rumble do her eyelids snap open. Unfocused, terror-filled eyes stare up at me.

"Dylan," she sighs when recognizes me, then lowers her

head to rest it against my pounding heart and goes back to sleep.

Fury washes over me. My wolf snarls and bares his fangs.

I vow to kill the fuckers who hurt my fated mate. Even if I have to die doing it. All of us will leave this Earth.

CHAPTER 9

asha

My heart races. My breath comes out in hot pants. The walls of my pussy contract as my back bows and toes curl. A heated flush spreads from my breasts up to my cheeks and down to my belly.

"*O, bogi!*"

My knees smash against together. A harsh grunt makes my eyes pop open. I drag myself up on an elbow and glance down my body.

Golden eyes gleam at me.

I fall to the pillow with a moan as I cum again at the vision of Dylan with his mouth pressed to my pussy and his eyes full of feral possession.

The mattress dips. He crawls over me, trailing wet

kisses along my belly to the undersides of my heaving breasts. His mouth engulfs as much of one ample breast as it can, then his cheeks hollow out to suckle the pebbled nipple.

I fist the longer hair on top of his head—unsure whether I want to pull him away or cradle him closer. Zings of passion course through me, increasing my sensitivity. I cry out his name.

"Yes, *Saaashaaa?*" Dylan teases and nips the pert tip. He quenches the fiery pain with gentle laps of his tongue. His lips drag across the valley between my breasts to lave the other nipple. "Do you want me to stop, Little Wolf?"

He snaps his hips to emphasize the question with his thick erection. It grows larger, wedged between us. Moisture from the tip coats my skin.

I mewl and shake my head vigorously. Then shudder at his roguish chuckle.

"I didn't think so."

Dylan continues until I'm a blubbering blob of jelly, begging him to fuck me. He leans on his haunches and lifts my hips, leaving my shoulders and head on the pillow. His ginormous cock aims for my entrance. Seeing it makes me wonder how it ever fit inside of me. The stretch and burn from last night remain.

"Don't worry, Little Wolf. They made you to fit every one of my inches inside your tight cunt."

My eyes flutter closed.

"Oh, no. Watch as your pussy swallows me whole."

I can't help but to obey. My eyes meet his, then slide

down his chiseled torso along the feathery plume of fine hair to his cock. The bulbous tip shines with pre-cum.

Slowly, it disappears as it breaches my slick folds. They part around him, gripping the length of velvet-covered steel. I hiss as the pain reignites.

Dylan pauses.

"Stay with me, Little Wolf. Pleasure will replace pain. Relax and let me in."

I glance at him. He's still. However, the veins in his neck and his fingertips digging into my butt cheeks prove it's an effort for him to hold back. Desire swirls in the depths of his golden eyes. I don't want him to hold back. I want him raw. With a deep inhalation, I will my body to release the tension.

"Good Little Wolf," Dylan purrs as his cock slips deeper within me. My abundant juices ease his passage. He groans and sucks his lower lip between his front teeth. His lusty gaze drawn to our carnal connection.

The tip of his cock brushes a spot on the upper wall of my core, and I gasp with a jerk. He groans deep in his throat and drags his cock out and thrusts forward, rubbing the spot.

"*Blyad'!*"

"Oh, Little Wolf, you don't know how good you feel squeezing cum from my cock. Now, take all of me."

Dylan slams into me, bottoming out at my cervix. I scream and dig my fingernails into his forearms. My entire body convulses with an orgasm. He rides me through it and the next two as he chases his release. His knot inflates, and I howl.

Head thrown back, he gives a mighty roar as his cock unleashes a torrent of hot cum into my womb. My pussy walls milk him until it draws every drop into me. His eyes smolder like the setting sun behind heavy lids as he watches me writhe in the tangle of silk sheets. The pressure of his knot proves unbearable.

"Easy, Little Wolf. Accept my knot. Fighting it increases the pain."

He lowers to his back with me draped over him. I whimper from the pull until we settle. His fingertips ghost along my sweat-dampened spine as he rumbles.

"Dylan, we need to talk."

His hand pauses as he stiffens.

I lift my cheek from his chest to look him in the eyes. He stares back at me.

"We're going to be laid up like this for a while. So now is a good time," I say and wait for a response. He cocks an eyebrow. I sigh and continue. "You claimed me without a conversation. You know more about me than I of you. Where's your pack? Will your parents accept me? Do you have siblings? What do you do besides fight? This is an expensive apartment. Your fighting affords it? Wha—"

"One question at a time, Sasha," he says, placing his index finger against my lips. "What do you want to know first?"

"Your pack. Tell me about them."

He sighs and closes his eyes. Time passes in silence. I

worry he won't answer. Then he opens his eyes and stares beyond my head.

"I don't have a pack anymore."

He pauses when I gasp in surprise.

"Yeah, I'm a rogue wolf. So, I won't blame you if you're pissed I claimed you, making you a rogue too. But I can take care of you better than a thousand packs put together."

I cup his cheek and shake my head.

"We'll get to the claiming in a minute. But I know you will take care of me no matter what. What happened with your pack to separate you?"

His eyes scan may face, then he kisses my palm.

"Oh, *Saaashaaa*. What you do to me…"

He tells me about growing up as the omega and being taunted, his friendship with the Alpha's son, and the challenge.

I sense he's always felt less than his best friends and lashes out to hide how he considers himself more brawn than brain. I admonished him when he referred to himself in that manner. But I didn't reveal my thoughts.

I'll help him realize he's so much more than the mindless beast people teased him as. It's one thing to use the moniker for the fight cage to intimidate opponents. But it's another to believe it applies in the rest of his life.

Then a sticky issue occurs to me.

"Does New York have a wolf pack? Did you speak to the Alpha about being in their territory?" I ask knowing my father would take offense if a wolf entered our pack lands uninvited. And for good reasons, as that horrific night proved.

Dylan sighs.

"Yes, and no. I bow to no one. I keep to myself. Garrett better not fuck with me."

His reaction worries me. If the Alpha finds out Dylan moved here, he'll consider it a challenge. And the outcome could prove disastrous. Somehow, I'll have to persuade Dylan to speak with the Alpha.

The vibrations of Dylan's rumble pull me from my thoughts. I glance at him.

"Relax, Sasha"—he brushes fingers over his mark—"Our mating bond allows us to sense the other's emotions. Do not worry. I mean what I say. You are safe with me, and I will care for you. That includes protecting you from any harm. Do you understand?"

I don't doubt him. But it's a tricky situation. Instead of protesting, I nod.

He cocks an eyebrow.

"Yes, Dylan, I understand."

He studies my face, then says, "Next question."

By the time he finishes answering my most-pressing questions, his knot deflates. I moan when he slips free. I'm so comfortable on him I'm reluctant to move. My arms wrap around his sides, and I burrow my face into his chest. His chuckle makes me giggle.

"Stay as you are, baby. We have more to talk about."

Now, I tense and pray he doesn't ask me about Kirill.

"You will tell me who hurt you. But I'll give you time to adjust to us first."

I sag in relief and press a kiss to his tattooed pec, then rub my cheek against his warm skin. Who knew having a mate could feel so good? I can't get enough of him.

"Easy, Little Wolf, or I'll fuck you hard again, whether or not your sore pussy protests."

Dylan's erotic threat makes my pussy flood with fresh arousal. He growls and smacks my ass. I yelp.

"Talk now. Fuck after. "

DYLAN

MY COCK TWITCHES from the jiggle of Sasha's round ass under my palm. For a moment, I'm tempted to pull her underneath me and fuck her into the mattress. My cock wants to stay inside of my fated mate. My wolf agrees.

But first we have shit to settle.

"You move in with me and quit your job at the diner."

She jumps up and stares at me as her mouth works. Her dove gray eyes darken to molten platinum. A flash of her wolf appears.

"Dylan! You can't just tell me what to do!"

I sit up and pull her into my lap. She struggles until I clasp her wrist and growl, sending my command through our mate bond. She stills. Eyes wide, she stares at me.

"Listen to me very carefully, Sasha. I *can* tell you what to do. I am your mate, the Alpha of our pack. What I say for you to do has a single purpose—your safety. If you should ever hesitate to obey me, you risk putting yourself in danger. I will not allow even *you* to prevent me from keeping you protected from harm. You are the daughter of an Alpha. You should know better. Do you understand?"

I hate to discipline Sasha, especially given her past. What they did to her was horrific. It was not done out of concern for her welfare. They had vicious intent, not for a lesson.

Again, she must be familiar with pack life order and the necessity for the Alpha to lead with a firm but fair hand. I must set clear expectations and explanations from the start. We have an unpredictable path ahead—the takedown of the wolf shifters who harmed her and Garrett's reaction to our presence included on it. Being rogue is difficult. And I need to be certain Sasha is with me in all ways.

She lowers her eyes in submission.

"I understand, Dylan. You are right. My father would agree with you. It's been me for so long, I forget how to rely on another. Please forgive me. We are our pack, and I willingly follow where you lead."

My heart swells with pride. I cup her beautiful face and slant my mouth over hers, then groan in satisfaction when her lips part to accept my probing tongue. It swoops through her mouth, tasting every corner before it tangles with hers for a dominating kiss.

Her submissive moans drive all blood to my cock. It

stands proud between us. She pulls from my mouth to stare from my erection to my face. She arches an eyebrow.

"Oh, don't think I forgot about you claiming me without—"

I silence her with my mouth on hers as I growl, "Sasha Vang, you are *mine* Forever!" Then roll her beneath me. I spend the next few hours teaching her not to question who she belongs to.

As we eat steaks delivered from Porter House on Columbus Circle, I smile. My Little Wolf chatters on about art classes she wants to take. When I asked her what she wants to do most in life, she responded to paint. She studied part-time at a university in St. Petersburg.

I told her even though I preferred she stayed home naked and ready for me, I promised we'd get her enrolled in the best school in New York City. In the meantime, we'll go to an art supply store and set up a studio for her in an unused room. We'll find a private tutor to train with until classes begin.

She squealed in delight and smothered me with kisses.

Then she called the diner and her roommates. To compensate for no notice, I offered two months' worth of her salary and rent. The cook said it was unnecessary, but I insisted. The roommates were happy for her and accepted. We will owe no one.

I sent a text message to Darrin Murray—my money manager—to wire the amounts and to arrange an AMEX black card along with bank accounts for Sasha. Like I do for my mother, he will transfer funds monthly and pay her expenses. Sasha will never worry about the cost of a damn thing. She can buy whatever the hell she wants.

She said she left nothing of value at the apartment, and the roommates would deal with the few items left. We'll go shopping for whatever she needs.

The one sticking point is her desire to continue volunteer work at the women's shelter. I reminded her how dangerous males—like the fighter—stalk females who flee from them. She gave me the side-eye and pointed out I did the same. Then collapsed into a fit of giggles as I pounced on her.

I compromised. If the shelter agrees to a security makeover I'll pay for, she can go, and I will escort her each time. She called Vera, who whooped and offered to speak with the director.

"Mmm mmm… Dylan! This golden sturgeon caviar is divine! You spoil me!"

"I'm glad you like it because the restaurant will deliver three meals a day for the next week while I keep you here in seclusion, *mate.*"

I smirk. If My Little Wolf thinks I spoil her with fish eggs, she ain't seen nothing yet. I'm hiring the best plastic surgeon in the world to remove that scar from her face. I'll stay in the operating room and collect all items used to prevent any of her blood getting into the wrong hands. No one can know about wolf shifters.

Once we finish the seclusion to complete our fated mate bond, Sasha will tell me who hurt her. And I will not compromise.

CHAPTER 10

asha

"WHEN WE GET in the park, I'll tell you when to shift. I'll scan the area to check for threats and humans who may be too close. And speaking of close. Stay at my side. Do not wander. Remain alert. If you notice something, poke my flank with your snout. Do you understand?"

Dylan fixes me with a dominant stare as his commands flow through our mating bond.

My wolf drops to her back and bares her throat and belly. I lower my gaze.

"Yes, My Alpha."

His rumble sends a shiver through me, and my nipples tighten beneath the t-shirt.

Tonight, is the first time we left his—I mean *our*, as

my fated mate reminds me—penthouse. Seven days of seclusion full of unquenchable fiery passion during which we explored each other's bodies, minds, and souls. The strength of our connection deepened in the first few days.

The ability for me to sense his happiness, concern, and most importantly, his love, fills me with joy. After the last year of hell, I never imagined I would find my fated mate and live the rest of my life in bliss. I thought my life was over when they killed my family and pack, then feared for it with Kirill.

Now, I have Dylan. Once again, I'm part of a true wolf shifter pack—albeit two of us. But we'll have plenty of pups if Dylan gets his way. And he will. Warmth fills my chest and my core.

"Fuck, *Saaashaaa*… I. Smell. You."

I lift my face as Dylan cuffs my neck and pulls me flush to his enormous body. His lips crash onto mine. He steals my breath as his demanding tongue possesses my mouth. Rising on tiptoe, I fist his t-shirt and grind against his burgeoning erection.

He moves us away from the street into the shadows of the park's entrance. Never does his mouth separate from mine. His tongue plunges deeper. He fucks my mouth.

I moan and wrap my leg around his hip. He grips my thigh and tips me backwards as he grinds his cock against my pussy. Only the thin fabric of my running shorts blocks him.

We lose ourselves to the passion that burns below the

surface. Even after hours of lovemaking over seven days, the urge to bond carnally runs high.

Dylan nips at my lower lip and draws it back. His eyes smolder like liquid gold. His wolf stares at me with lust. My lip pops from his teeth. I lick it with the tip of my tongue. He growls as his eyes flash.

"Unless you want me to fuck you right here and not run, we better stop now, Little Wolf."

For a moment, I'm tempted to turn tail and race to our building, knowing he'd give chase. But I haven't run free in a year. My wolf whines and paces, eager to come forth.

"You tempt me, My Alpha. But my wolf needs to run free. It's been far too long."

He nods and takes my hand to lead us to the path lined by ornate wrought-iron lampposts. We walk in silence. He scans our surroundings for threats while I absorb its beauty.

Stone walls darkened by age mark the perimeter. Pillars flank the entrance we slipped through. Along the cobblestone path, green benches stand before the grassy areas where an abundance of trees rise to the inky, starless night sky.

Raccoons climb on trashcans in search of scraps. The little bandits lift their gazes from foraging to watch two lethal predators. They detect our wolves. Once we pass, the raccoons return to their dinner.

Rustling within the leaves of a nearby elm tree draws my attention. I narrow my gaze to pinpoint the source. Red furry bodies extend wings. A colony of red bats awake from their slumber to hunt. Not a fan of the creatures, I turn my attention to the left.

Across the asphalt concrete drive, another grassy, tree-filled area stretches to a large pond. Its surface ripples with the breeze. Ducks huddle in nests gathered in bushes along its edge. Beaks appear from beneath their back feathers as they sense our wolves, too.

Dylan squeezes my hand, and I glance up at him. He tilts his chin towards a cluster of trees beyond the pond. I follow as he changes direction. When we reach the center hidden by low branches, he drops his black backpack to the grass.

"We'll shift here. You first. Our clothes will go in the backpack. Before I shift, I'll put it on. Remember to always stay by my side, Sasha. Now, hand me your clothes and sneakers. Then shift."

My wolf drops her front legs and raises her rear, tail wagging. She's ready to play, and so am I!

I peel off the t-shirt. My full breasts bounce free. The already puckered nipples tighten to peaks as the cool air licks at them. I toe off the sneakers. My hips shimmy as I slip out of the shorts. When I rise with the clothes bundled in my arms, Dylan stares at me. My cheeks flush crimson from his unleashed desire.

A needy whine rises in the back of my throat. He growls in response and stalks towards me. My clothes fall to the ground. Once again, he kisses me senseless. He pulls away, and my body leans towards him, drawn like a magnet to steel. Or rather to his velvet-covered steel rod that tents his shorts.

"I'm not waiting until we get back, Little Wolf."

I squeeze my thighs together as my fingernails dig into his forearms. *O, bogi!* Does he mean to mount me in wolf form? My wolf leaps to her feet and howls.

"Shift, *mate.*"

Dylan's command catches me off guard, but not my wolf. She surges forward at our Alpha's command. Bones reshape and muscles lengthen as I shift to my white blonde wolf. Amidst crackling and a flash, we stand on four legs moments later. My fur-covered head tilts back to gaze at our Alpha.

"So beautiful you are, my mate. Gorgeous," he murmurs as he circles me, trailing his fingertips along my neck and flank. The feathery edges of my tail slip through his fingers. They move to caress my spine and the top of my head. The pad of his thumb brushes the fur-less scar. I duck.

"Oh, no, Little Wolf. You will not hide your face from me. No scar can lessen your beauty," he says as he crouches in front of me and cups my jaw. "Now, I'll shift, and we'll run. Then mate."

My fur ripples as I shudder. *Yes!*

Dylan strips and adds his clothes with mine to the backpack. He loosens the straps, then loops his arms through. It hangs to the side. Moments later, it fits snug to his massive black wolf. The same wolf from my dreams. My fantasy lover come to life.

Slowly, I approach him with my head and tail low. My wolf wants to guarantee he sees we pose no threat. We are omega to his Alpha. I pause at a low growl. A tentative step forward elicits another low growl. Immediately, I drop to the ground and bare my throat and belly.

He pads forward and nuzzles my vulnerable areas. Hot breath blows my fur as he sniffs and chuffs.

I remain completely still.

He probes between my rear legs and rumbles. The flat of his textured tongue laves my sensitive bits.

I whimper.

He growls low in his throat.

A nip to my flank breaks my stillness. I yelp and gaze up at him. Tempered lust fills his eyes. He jerks his head, and I roll to all fours. A quick shake loosens the leaves and twigs stuck to my fur. He pads from beneath the branches. I follow.

We run and play through Central Park, staying in the shadows. The scent of fresh grass, musky-sweetness of fallen leaves, squirrels asleep in their burrows, and unbathed humans flow through the crisp air past my nose. The pads of my feet snap twigs and grip boulders with every bounding step. My heart races as fast as my legs. Free!

Dylan slows and lopes towards a rock formation. He pauses outside the opening and blocks me from following. He steps inside. Seconds later, his head peeks out. He rumbles and steps back. I enter. My eyes dart around the cave.

Dirt covers the ground with windswept leaves scattered about. The rough surface of the rocks creates three walls and a ceiling. Away from the chill, the temperature is comfortable—not that wolf shifters get cold. It's cozy.

Dylan prods me with his snout and shrugs his shoulders. I nod and use my teeth to tug the backpack straps from his body. I watch it drop to the ground. When my gaze lifts, Dylan stares at me like a hungry predator ready to devour its prey.

DYLAN

MY FATED MATE'S scent taunted my nostrils from the moment we stood outside of Central Park. Many times, I had to fight the urge to push her against a tree and plunge my hungry cock deep into her cunt.

But she told me how much she misses running as a wolf as she did through her Russian pack's ancestral lands. Her face glowed with pure happiness as she described the grassy knolls, windy cliffs above the Gulf of Finland, and the snowy forests.

I promised I'd take her back soon. She teared up and said she would be grateful for a chance to pray for her family and friends on their lands. If there's anything salvageable, we'll bring it with us.

Central Park offers her the chance to reconnect with

nature in the middle of Manhattan. Even if we can't run during the day, our enhanced vision allows us to enjoy it at night.

And now, I wish to take pleasure in my fated mate. My wolf howls in agreement.

I prowl towards her—a constant rumble in my chest. She remains still. I breathe in her unique scent as once again I nuzzle her neck, flank, and base of tail. With a possessive growl, I rise onto my hind legs and wrap my front ones around her waist and legs. My thighs bracket hers.

She lifts her tail.

I plunge my aching cock inside of her. She whines and stamps her front feet. I growl as my hips pump vigorously. Nips to her neck and shoulders still her wriggling. My knot expands. Her pussy contracts. She paws the ground, whining as we lock together. I rumble in my chest to soothe her while we remain carnally connected.

Fifteen minutes later, my knot deflates, and we separate. I nuzzle her flank and lick her snout. She returns my affection.

I step away and send my contented wolf back to the fringes of my being. He retreats at my will. On all fours, I stretch and watch as my beautiful mate shifts. I look forward to more of her white blonde wolf.

"Oh, My Alpha, thank you," she purrs as she stretches. "I feel amazing, my love."

She presses her forehead against mine. A yawn interrupts our moment of bliss. She giggles and reaches for the backpack. Handing my clothes to me, she smiles.

"It's been a while since I've been so… active."

Kneeling, I chuckle and tug my t-shirt over my head. When we're dressed, I crawl out our den and scan the area. Sasha crawls forward and slips her hand in mine. She stifles another yawn.

"Come. We'll take a cab home, Little Wolf. I'll bathe you and tuck you in for a good night's sleep. I have surprises for you tomorrow."

She bounces on the balls of her feet and kisses my cheek.

Who knew I'd fall so hard for a fated mate I didn't believe in?

CHAPTER 11

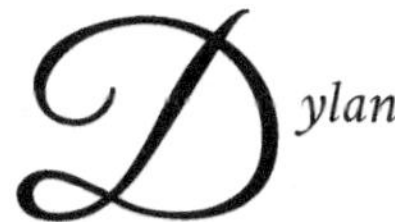ylan

"Dylan, this is too much! I was doing fine with my disposable mobile. I don't need a fancy iPhone. Nor the fancy iPad, watch, and laptop! Okay, well, the laptop will be useful for my schoolwork. But the other stuff?"

Sasha sits cross-legged on the living room floor surrounded by boxes from Apple. Her eyebrows scrunch as she glances from one to the next. The building's porter delivered them a few minutes ago. Part of my day of surprises for her.

I lean over and pick up the iPhone. Pressing the button to activate it.

"You're not listening to me, Dylan," she huffs and reaches for the device. Her hand yanks back at my growl.

"Did we not have the conversation about you obeying me, Little Wolf?"

She gapes. Her eyes flick from my face to the iPhone, then to the rest. She folds her arms across her breasts and lifts her chin.

"Yes, we did, I'll give you the mobile. But how do the laptop, iPad, and watch protect me?"

She has me there. But I won't admit it. I continue to tap on the mobile screen.

"Ha! Got you! You can't answer because you know they don't."

I lift my gaze and smirk.

"Besides its health and emergency alerts, the Apple Watch serves as a phone if you're out for a run and don't have the iPhone. The laptop keeps your information safe as opposed to you using a public computer at school. The iPad replaces the laptop when you don't want to carry the larger one with your schoolbooks and art supplies."

Sasha shakes her head. Tendrils from the bun on top sway.

When we're home, she's not self-conscious about the scar and wears her hair in a bun or a braid. It makes me happy she's comfortable with me seeing her full face. Although, I love her waist-long hair loose. I like to run my fingers through it as she rests her head in my lap. Or fist it when we fuck.

"Dylan, you're too much," she giggles, then crawls over to straddle me and wraps her arms around my neck. "Thank you, my love."

My love.

Yeah. Every time she says it, my heart clenches.

To think I was hellbent on denying us as fated mates because I didn't believe in them. It makes me wonder if Jagger ever found his true one. If he did, good for him. He knew from the start he wouldn't settle for anything less. Now I know why he was so adamant. I can't imagine myself with any she-wolf but Sasha. Mine!

"You're welcome, baby," I respond and kiss the tip of her nose. She giggles and nuzzles my cheek. "Let me finish activating your iPhone and watch. We have an appointment in thirty minutes."

She leans to stare at me, arms draped on my shoulders.

"For what? Is it outside?"

"A surprise and yes," I respond as I scoot her from my lap. "Why don't you dress while I finish?"

Her dove gray eyes sparkle like diamonds. Gracefully, she rises to her feet. A kiss to the crown of my head, and she skips from the living room.

I bring them with me to our bedroom suite. Sasha's still in the shower. I stare at the door, then my watch. No time. I change into a black v-neck cashmere sweater, dark denim jeans, and heavy boots.

"I'm ready."

Sasha stands in the doorway of my dressing room. When she ordered clothes from online, she picked some basics. She chose the gray sweater, black jean, and black heeled boots for our outing. She holds a black wool coat.

I keep a straight face, even though I want to punch a

hole in the wall at the sight of her hair pulled over her shoulder to cover the side of her face. Others may think it's a style. I know it's hiding the scar. I swear I'm going to the *kill* those fuckers!

Our seclusion ended. But I don't want to ruin her surprises for today and tomorrow. The day after, it's confession time. She will tell me the names and where to find them.

"You okay?"

The red haze clears from my vision. Sasha frowns at me and instinctively pulls the hair closer to her face. Fuck! I forgot about the mate bond.

I take a deep breath and mentally shake off the murderous thoughts. Patience.

"Come, baby, let's go," I say as I grab my leather motor-cycle jacket and take her hand. I kiss her knuckles and lead her to our private elevator.

She's quiet.

I tap into the bond to figure what emotion she feels. Hurt. Damn! I slam the emergency stop button and cage her in the corner as the elevator jolts. My eyes line up with hers.

"What's wrong, Little Wolf? And do not tell me nothing."

She blinks and glances away. I tsk, and she meets my gaze.

"Are you... embarrassed to go out with me because... because of my... the scar?"

With a growl, I spin away. My fists dent the wall panel.

Sasha gasps.

"Mr. Vang, are you all right, sir? The emergency—"

"Yes! Give us a minute!" I bellow towards the intercom, then I face Sasha.

Her one visible eye shines with unshed tears. She blinks, and they fall down her unblemished cheek.

My heart breaks. I grind my molars to bite back a snarl. I want to rage. Rip something apart. But I can't. I've already upset her. With her recent feistiness, I forget she's still so fragile.

"Baby. I love you. All of you. Each and every inch," I say as I push her hair aside and press my lips to the jagged scar. "Nothing can take away your beauty. If either of us should be embarrassed, it's you for being with a beast like me. I don't deserve you, Sasha Vang. But you can't get rid of me now, baby. I'm yours, and you're mine. Forever. Do you understand?"

She swallows and nods.

I let her non-verbal answer go uncorrected. She's too upset. Instead of demanding she open her mouth to speak, I cover it with mine and kiss her until she sags against me. I trail kisses over the scar and bury my face in her hair. Her scent calms my beast.

"As much as I want to take you back upstairs and tie you to the bed and fuck you for hours, we have to go."

She nods and rubs her hands over my back, beneath my jacket. Her gentle touch calms me further.

I press a last kiss to her cheek and press the emergency stop button. The elevator descends. I keep her caged in the corner, kissing her face until we reach the lobby. She fixes her hair over her cheek and gives me a small smile. I cup her chin and press my forehead to hers.

"Forever, My Little Wolf."

"Forever, My Alpha."

We stop by the concierge desk for me to tell them I'll pay for the damage to our elevator. Then we head out for Fifth Avenue.

Mr. Smooth Dresser Bennett told me Bergdorf Goodman has everything a stylish woman could need for a new wardrobe. "From lingerie to the coat and shoes with bags to match. Only the best!"

I booked a half-day appointment with their top consultant and sent a photo of Sasha with sizes from her other clothes. Ruby promised to help her select clothes and accessories for every occasion. We'll break for lunch. Then meet her for fittings. They'll deliver everything to our penthouse.

We hurry since we have five minutes to get there. I don't want Sasha to miss a minute. People turn to complain when I weave through the crowds. Then turn away hastily when they see a six-foot-seven-inch beast towering over them. And Sasha thought *she* embarrassed *me*...

She giggles and tells me to stop bowling them over. I shrug. They need to move the hell out of the way. My fated mate needs some clothes.

We reach the northwest corner of Fifth-eighth Street and Fifth Avenue. Bergdorf's—as Bennett calls it—stands across the street. The window displays show snazzy dresses. So, I guess it'll live up to the hype. The light changes, and we surge ahead of the crowd, straight to the revolving door.

"We're going in here?" Sasha asks as I put her ahead of me and push the brass pole.

"Surprise," I respond as we shuffle along. It's a close fit, with my bulky frame bent over her smaller one.

The doorman greets us with a tip of his hat. Sasha smiles, and I nod, then glance around. Ruby said she'd meet us at the door.

A well-dressed human female in her forties approaches us, her green eyes on Sasha.

"You must be Mrs. Vang. Welcome to Bergdorf Goodman," she says as she extends her hand. "I'm Ruby, your wardrobe consultant."

Sasha glances up at me, and I nod. She stretches her hand out. Ruby takes it and smiles.

"You're more stunning in person. Your hair and eye colors are so rare," she says, then looks up at me. "Mr. Vang, a pleasure to meet you in person. Kindly come me."

She guides us to elevators, pointing out areas of the store—jewelry, accessories, and handbags on this level, beauty one below. We ride up in silence with others. Once the doors open on the floor she selected, Ruby rambles on again. She turns into a hallway and opens a door.

We step inside. I'm thankful to see a couch. Yes, I want to spoil Sasha. But I sure as hell don't want to run around shopping all day. I pull out my mobile and hunker down.

SASHA

I've been to shops in St. Petersburg for jeans, sweaters, basic stuff. But nothing like this. The store oozes glamour. The patrons look like they stepped off the pages of *Vogue*! Too worried I don't fit in I barely listen to Ruby. I'm a simple she-wolf raised in the rural area outside of a city. Plus, I want to fall through the floor with this nasty scar blazoned across my cheek.

But the happiness in Dylan's eyes at his surprise stops me from running straight to his—I mean *our*—penthouse. I take a deep breath.

"Would you care for some coffee, tea, or water, Mrs. Vang, Mr. Vang?"

Mrs. Vang... It surprised me when Ruby addressed me as such. Dylan must have told her we're married. He refers to me as Mrs. Vang, but I didn't think he'd do so to others. Not that I mind. I'm proud to bear his name. My fated mate and My Alpha. I love him so much.

"Tea would be lovely, thank you, Ruby." I respond while Dylan asks for water.

Ruby picks up a phone and places our orders, then returns to my side.

"May I have your coat? We'll go through the plan for today. How does that sound, Mrs. Vang?"

"Wonderful, thank you. Although, I must admit I'm a bit

overwhelmed"—my eyes dart to Dylan, and I smile—"I mean, I'm happy with my surprise. It's just I've never been amongst such luxury."

Ruby's warm smile puts me at ease. She tells me we have several hours together and lunch. An assistant appears with a tray. I thank him and sip my tea while I sit next to Dylan and listen to Ruby. By the time she's finished, I'm excited to start.

In the dressing room, I change into a platinum silk kimono. When I re-enter the main room, roll-away racks filled with dresses line one wall. Ruby stands beside them, smiling at me.

I feel like Cinderella getting dressed by her fairy godmother!

I clap my hands and kiss Dylan on my way to Ruby. He whispers, I love you, and I nuzzle his cheek.

The next few hours pass in a blur of dresses and pants and blouses for daytime, mini dresses for nights outs, and lingerie and loungewear. Dylan lets us know his opinion with a firm no or a nod. Most of the mini dresses switch to an inch above the knee. I laugh at my possessive fated mate.

I try on lace and silk bras, corsets, slips, and negligees. He doesn't have to nod to let me know he approves. I sense his lust through our mate bond. Mobile cast aside, he stares at me with hungry eyes. My nipples bead against the soft fabrics.

Ruby holds up a stunning nightgown with sheer white lace panels for the breasts and pearl silk from the waist to the ankle-length hem. The distraction breaks the lustfest.

Hours later, the clothes get whisked away for alterations. Assistants enter with trolleys of handbags and shoes. I pick up a pair of sparkly stilettos. Now, I really feel like Cinderella! I try them on first. Ruby says they'll complement the Swarovski Crystal embellished evening gown I fell in love with. I don't know where I'll wear it, but I couldn't resist it. And Dylan approved with a broad smile since it hugs my ass.

After we make my selections, I put my sweater and jeans back on. Ruby escorts us to BG Restaurant and says she'll return in an hour. The host leads us to a table by the windows with views of Central Park. I grin at Dylan, remembering the incredible night we spent. He winks.

"How are you enjoying your surprise, baby?"

I reach across the white-linen-covered table and squeeze his hand.

"Oh, Dylan! I love it! I feel like Cinderella transformed after a year of drudgery. This is one of the best days of my life. Thank you, my love!"

He grins and rises from his chair to kiss me across the table. His tongue dives into my mouth. Each sweep of his tongue contracts my core. This male! I can't resist him. He nips my lower lip before he sits.

"The pleasure is all mine, *Saaashaaa.*"

A server appears for our order. I ask his recommendation and choose their famous Gotham Salad. Dylan orders the filet of beef.

"The dresses and pants with blouses are perfect for my volunteer work, and I'll wear the jeans and sweaters to class. Even the party dresses make sense if we go to a club. But when will I wear the formal gowns? Are you sure I need them?"

Dylan raises his hand to stop my questions.

"Who knows? I find it best to be ready than to scramble about at the last minute. But if you'd rather go without the clothes—"

I shake my head like crazy.

"Oh, no! I want them!"

"More than me?"

Oh, my possessive fated mate...

CHAPTER 12

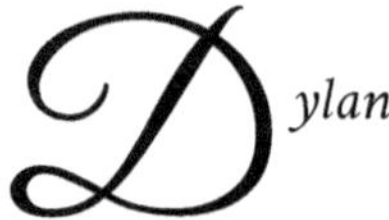ylan

"Do you trust me?"

Sasha's dove gray eyes stare up at me with eyebrows raised. She flicks her uncertain gaze from my face to the blindfold in my hand. She worries her lower lip with her teeth as she considers my question.

I know she trusts me. But it's odd to ask her to wear a blindfold while we stand on the southwest corner of Fifty-seventh Street and Seventh Avenue in the middle of the morning. People hustle past us on the busy corner. I wait patiently.

She inhales and brings her gaze back to my face.

"Yes, My Alpha, I trust you. It's just weird you want me to put that on here," she says as she glances around and pats her hair. "People will look at me funny. And I don't want them to see the scar."

I press my forehead to hers.

"Baby, I will never expose the scar. I'll be careful. But if you don't want to wear the blindfold, you'll have to keep your eyes closed for your surprise. The choice is yours."

Her hand cups my cheek as she says, "I'll wear the blindfold, my love. I don't want to ruin your surprise."

She closes her eyes, and I place the black silk over them and tell her to hold it in place while I tie it behind her head. I adjust her hair to remain over her cheek beneath the silk. Then I wrap my arm around her waist, hugging her close to my side as I lead her along the street.

It's not long before we reach the building. I place Sasha in front of me with my hands on her shoulders.

"We're here. I'll take the blindfold off," I murmur in her ear. "Ready?"

"Yes, my love," she whispers as she holds her hair in place. Her excitement rolls down our mate bond as her heart beats faster. "But where are we?"

I point across the street to the four-story French Renaissance style stone building—the website explained its history. Ornate stonework decorates the edges of the windows and cornice. On the ground floor, four oversized plate-glass windows display paintings. A navy blue canopy marks its entrance.

"The Art Students League of New York?" Sasha asks in wonder as she reads the gold letters above the arched entry.

"Surprise, baby."

She whoops and spins around. Her arms fly around my neck as she bounces on the balls of her feet. Her dove gray eyes shine with glee.

"Yesterday, a whole new wardrobe. Today, art classes? Dylan Vang, you spoil me! Thank you, my love!"

She presses kisses all over my face as I chuckle and hold her close. The alert on my iPhone dings. Time for our appointment. I take Sasha's hand and wait for the traffic to stop, then dash across the street. She giggles, running beside me. We continue up the stairs leading to the front doors.

A man with gray hair and glasses approaches us.

"Mr. and Mrs. Vang?" When we confirm, he continues with a smile. "Welcome to The Art Students League of New York! I am Antonio Diaz, the Artistic/Executive Director. Mrs. Vang, your husband tells me you're a painter and wish to continue your studies."

Sasha grins and shakes his hand.

"Yes. But please call me Sasha."

He nods and shakes my hand. I tell him to call me Dylan. He gives us a tour before we meet in his office. He explains their one-hundred-fifty-year history and their fine art certificate program. A few instructors and staff members stop in to speak with Sasha.

She tells them about her studies in St. Petersburg and what she wants to do. I sit back in the chair and watch as she practically bursts with excitement. She's so focused on her dream, she doesn't notice her hair moves out of place.

I scan the others' faces. But they don't react. Good for them, or I'd rip them apart and use their limbs to paint the walls with their blood. Call me Picasso.

"You should model too. Your beauty is extraordinary. Your hair and eyes. The angles of your face—"

"Watch yourself," I growl. The memory of the woman in a studio lying naked on a sofa in front of students—including males—pops into my mind. Not my fated mate!

Sasha puts her hand on my thigh and rubs the taut muscles, ready for me to pounce on the fucker.

"Please excuse, Richard. He will apologize," Antonio says quickly and cocks an eyebrow at the man.

He raises his hands, palms out. "I apologize. I meant no disrespect. As an artist, I train my eye to recognize the potential for a masterpiece. Please forgive me."

I scan his face and scent the air for lies. Even though I find none, I glare at him when I nod.

"Apology accepted. Just don't get any ideas, artist or not."

"Thank you, Richard," Antonio says to dismiss him. He scurries out the door, shutting it behind him firmly. "I will speak with him. I hope his behavior will not dissuade you from joining our program."

Antonio looks at me as he speaks.

I turn to Sasha and ask, "Are you comfortable?"

"Absolutely. I'm sure he understands the boundaries," she answers, then shifts her gaze to Antonio. "And I'll apply as soon as we get home. I want to start with the next semester."

"Wonderful! That's all for today. I'll walk you to our art supply store. The manager expects you and will help you select what you need for your home studio."

"It just gets better!" Sasha exclaims.

"Surprise," I say with a grin.

I promised we'd get her enrolled in the best school in New York City and set up a studio in an unused room. Antonio suggested Sasha paints as she has without a private tutor, so she starts the program free of any recent training.

She's happier than a kid in a candy store as she chatters with the manager. Since she knew we were coming and what Sasha needed, the manager goes to each section to show Sasha her options. Her wide eyes take in the assortment of brushes, easels, paints, and whatever else a painter needs. I trail behind happy she's happy.

Sasha spies the gift section and "can't resist a peek." She picks out artsy books she says we can put on the coffee tables. She's adding her touches to make it our home. And it pleases me to no end.

Ninety minutes later, she hands her AMEX black card to the manager.

"Looks like you broke the bank, baby."

She gasps as rosy pink blossoms on her alabaster cheeks.

I grab her in my arms and bury my face in her neck, chuckling.

"Oh, Dylan! I thought you were mad. Don't tease me like that. Gah!" She says as she fists my sweater.

The manager laughs and waits for me to release Sasha, then returns her AMEX.

"You're a lucky girl, Sasha! The guys will bring everything and set up your studio in an hour. Is that good for you?"

"I am, and yes, thank you! See you in a couple of months," Sasha responds as I drag her from the store.

An hour? Just enough time to take my payment.

SASHA

"Now, ain't that a pretty picture?"

I jolt at Dylan's unexpected baritone—sexily husky by sleep—breaks the early morning silence. He leans in the doorway of my studio with his hands braced on the top of the doorframe. Drool-worthy biceps, pecs, and abs flex. Black joggers skim his narrow hips. The impressive bulge of his cock rests along his muscular thigh.

With a smirk at my slack jaw, he pads towards me on bare feet.

"How did you sneak out of bed without waking me, naughty Little Wolf?"

He drops his hands on the chrome-plated steel armrests of my white leather artist's chair and spins me around. His face inches away from mine. Our lips a hair's breadth apart.

"Do I need to tie you to the posts?"

I shiver. The thin cotton of Dylan's undershirt I snagged to wear while I paint does little to hide my peaked nipples. My pussy clenches beneath the skimpy shorts. Instant arousal floods my core. A moan slips from my mouth.

"Mmmmmm," he purrs. "Is that your answer, naughty Little Wolf? I think I like it and want to hear more…"

He strides forward, pushing the chair away from the easel where a fresh canvas rests with the beginnings of my charcoal sketch. The chair stops in the middle of the north-facing corner room. Sunlight streams through the walls of windows, highlighting Dylan's angular face. For a moment, it distracts me, and I consider how I would paint his masculine beauty.

But then he lowers to his knees between my spread thighs.

The charcoal falls from my fingers to the hardboard-covered floor.

"Delicious, Little Wolf," he murmurs as his nose brushes the seat of my shorts. "And bare for me. What a good girl."

I mewl and rock my hips, grinding against him wantonly.

He chuckles and nips at my distended clit. My yelp morphs into a moan as he sucks the pain away.

"We don't need these now, do we?"

The shorts follow the charcoal.

His tongue licks the seam of my lower lips. A groan mixes with a growl as his tongue plunges between my slick folds. I grip the armrests and close my eyes to relish in his feasting.

Skilled tongue, teeth, and fingers combine for mind-blowing orgasms. I lose count after the first two. The aftershocks of the last blends into next for a continuous climax. Throat raw from my screams, I sag limp in the chair.

"My turn."

Dylan levers the chair to its highest setting. The mushroom head of his cock perfectly aligns to my pussy. He puts my calves on his broad shoulders. Once again, he grips the armrests. However, the chair slides forward. His cock penetrates my pussy in one brutal stroke as his ball sac slaps my bottom hole.

I keen at the massive invasion. It triggers another orgasm. My legs quiver and toes curl. Not only does he blow my mind, it short circuits.

He reaches down and rips the front of my t-shirt. The pieces slide apart to reveal my heavy breasts and achy nipples. His mouth lowers to latch onto one.

Moans pour from my slack mouth with each strong pull. My fingernails dig into his corded forearms. I writhe when my nipple pops from his mouth.

The chair rolls away from him. His engorged cockhead brushes my swollen folds. The chair returns to position, and I keen again. Dylan continues to hammer my ravaged pussy between suckling my sore breasts. I can only hang on and go along for the carnal ride.

His dick grows in girth. Gripped in his sizable hands, the chair rolls back and forth so quickly I fear it may break.

The sound of the steel wheels on the hardboard like a saw through wood. I hold tight to his forearms as my legs slide up and down either side of his head.

Golden feral eyes gleam. Sweat beads at his hairline. His tan skin flush.

A final roll and penetration, and Dylan's eyes roll to the back of his head. Thick veins rise in his neck. He throws his head back and howls to the ceiling. It ends in a low and guttural groan.

My pussy floods with copious amounts of his hot seed. A final orgasm has me joining in his feral howl. My sweat-drenched body convulsing. My mind fractures. Euphoria washes over me.

The chair slows as his thrusts ease to a lazy pace. He grunts in male satisfaction.

I regain consciousness as he carries me into our white marble bathroom. The vibrations of his rumbling along with the strength of his heartbeat pulsate beneath my ear. I nuzzle against his chest with a languorous sigh.

"Feel good, baby?"

"Mmmm. Indeed, my love. That was the best painting session I ever had."

His chuckle blends with the beat of his heart.

"Glad to hear it. That chair is as good as a swing,"

I lift my head to gaze at him, eyebrow raised in question.

"Ah, my innocent Little Wolf. A sex swing where the receiver remains strapped into a swing made of sturdy cloth suspended from the ceiling while the giver pulls it back and forth to mount them. Like I did with you in your chair."

"I like the sound of that," I say with a giggle. Better than breaking my chair or cutting a hole in the floor!

Dylan chuckles wickedly and says, "You've given me an idea for another surprise…"

My body heats, and I stifle a moan. I'll never get enough of this male!

He bathes me in the shower and washes my hair. I do the same for him. Cocooned in comfy terrycloth robes, we eat omelets I cook.

When I saw the top-of-the-line chef's kitchen, I told Dylan I would cook at least one meal a day for us. I couldn't believe he touched none of the gadgets and appliances except for the refrigerator and microwave.

"What's the plan for today?" I ask as we sit at the pale gray leather banquette in the eating nook.

"I say we stay in for a mini seclusion. Tomorrow, it's back to the real world. We go to the women's shelter for the security makeover. You can hang out with Vera while I watch the installations. Sounds good, baby? Or do you want to do something else?"

I take the last bite of my omelet and jump up from the bench.

"I say let's start now. That is, if you can catch me," I respond.

With a wink, I untie the sash of my robe and let it drop to the floor, then dash from the kitchen. My bare feet slap on the hardwood floor.

Dylan roars.

I shudder in anticipation of him catching me. But I increase my speed to a full run. My fleeing will ignite the predator in him. I hope he'll mount me as his wolf.

I hear him closing in on me as I round the corner, headed for our bedroom suite. I call forth my wolf. She bursts forth and bounds through the open double doors.

Dylan howls. His wolf clear in his rugged voice. His paw swipes my rear leg, and I tumble to the floor. He pounces. We roll around, crashing into the sitting room coffee table. Soon, our affectionate play transforms into carnal pleasure. Life can't get better than this!

I just pray when we re-enter the real world, our happy bubble doesn't burst.

CHAPTER 13

asha

"SASHA! How fantastic you look! Girl, you're glowing! I love your coat. Rick Owens?"

Vera holds me from her at arm's length. Her hazel eyes roam from my head to my toes. Then she pulls me in for another hug.

"It feels as though we haven't seen each other in months!" She glances over at Dylan, who greeted her, then went to speak with the installation crew. "That bad boy is rocking your world, huh?"

We fall out in giggles. She loops her arm through mine, and we head to her office, chatting the entire way. I put my coat and handbag in her closet, and she locks the office door.

"The security makeover thrilled the director. We called the police two days ago to remove an ex-husband from the front steps. When we wouldn't let him in, he broke the intercom with the butt of a handgun! I had to convince Liza it wasn't her fault. Fortunately, the pro bono attorney drafted a protective order..."

Vera brings me up to date as we walk to the cafeteria to help distribute lunch. I say a silent prayer of thanks Dylan insisted they accept his generous donation. It'll help keep the women and the staff safe. One security guard and a camera with an intercom at the front door don't provide enough protection. Plus, Dylan would never allow me to continue my volunteer work without it, especially after the gun incident. I'm nervous about mentioning it to him.

Along the way to the cafeteria, a few residents stop us to chat. They're happy to see me and thought I quit. I assure them I'm here for good. When I tell them I was on my honeymoon, they hug and congratulate me.

Vera arches an elegant eyebrow, and I smile.

"Okay, that's news to me, *bestie*..." she says once we're alone. Her heart-shaped face crumples in disappointment. "Why didn't you tell me the big boy and you married?"

I grab her in a big hug. It's so nice to have a girlfriend again. I miss my friends from Russia and the she-wolves in Pennsylvania.

"We didn't officially marry. We agreed to be life partners. If we were to marry, I'd tell my absolute best friend first! And ask you to be my maid of honor."

Vera's shoulders lose the tension, and she squeezes me tight.

"Oh, good! I thought you wouldn't want me there, and I couldn't understand why not."

I assure her she was mistaken. The moment passes, and we reach the cafeteria.

Inside, volunteers stand behind the counter scooping tuna salad onto lettuce or buns and vegetable soup into cups. My wolf senses detect the lunch offerings even from this distance. The residents line up at the counter or eat at round metal tables with matching chairs. Some residents gather with others while a few sit alone.

Despite the sunny yellow paint, the cafeteria still resembles a cold institution. It's clean but needs freshening up. Vinyl tile floors scuffed by the feet of the chair legs need repair. Harsh fluorescent lighting dulls everyone's faces. Even those who laugh appear sad.

"Vera, I have an idea."

She turns to me as we put on our aprons, hairnets, and gloves.

"I'd like to give the shelter a comfy home makeover. The security updates will protect the residents and staff. But everyone would feel more at ease if the shelter didn't feel cold and institutional."

I share my thoughts, and Vera agrees. Funding concerns her since they use most of the donations and grants for residents' programs to help them adjust to life after the shelter. When I tell her I'll ask Dylan, she hesitates since he's paying a hefty amount for the security. But I know he'll do it for me. So, I tell her not to worry and to get the director's approval. Vera agrees.

While we serve lunch, I tell her the residents can help to paint murals I sketch in the cafeteria and other areas of the shelter. It will give them a chance to express their artistic sides and complement the programs. Who knows? We may have another Olga Rozanova in our midst!

Our excitement for the makeover stays with us for the rest of the day. In between workshops, we think of other comforts of home we can bring into the shelter. By the time Dylan calls my mobile, Vera and I have a solid plan. We set it aside and head to the reception area to meet Dylan and the director.

As I turn the corner, Dylan already stares in my direction. His nostrils flare, and I know he scented me well before I came into view. A flash of his wolf appears in his golden eyes as he eats up the sight of me.

I bite the corner of my lower lip as I attempt to push the instant craving for my fated mate to the side. We need to concentrate and not get lost in our carnal desires. At least until we return home!

"Hi, baby, I missed you," he says as his arm reaches around for my hip to pull me against his side. He lowers his voice so only I can hear. "My cock throbs for your sweet little pussy. When I get you home, I'm going to fuck you until *I* can't walk."

He squeezes my hip bone, and I bite back a squeal. Then he nuzzles my neck and presses a kiss behind my ear. He glances at a human male and nods.

No one dares to comment on his public display of affection. Except Vera, who grins and winks at me. Dylan chuckles and pulls me tighter against his side.

The male heads the installation team. He explains the state-of-the-art security system and walks us through the shelter. They installed cameras, locks on all exterior doors, intercoms for the front door and for the main rooms to the offices, and panic buttons in key locations. The director expresses thanks for the extensive system, and the team leaves.

"Dylan, we truly appreciate your generous donation. The new system will make an enormous difference in the level of safety for our residents and our staff. Especially after the incident the other day."

Dylan stiffens and barks, "What incident?"

The director startles. She glances from Dylan to Vera and back.

"Uh... A resident's ex-husband tried to enter with a handgun..."

When she finishes, a bone-chilling silence descends. Anger radiates off Dylan. It scorches along our mate bond. I rub my chest from the searing pain of it.

"Sasha, get your things."

My mouth gapes as I stare up at him.

He narrows his eyes imperceptibly. His wolf close to the surface.

"Dylan, the police arrested him, and a restraining order was obtained. He's no longer a threat. We're safe, even more so now," the director adds quickly.

"The security system will protect as much as it can," he says, then turns to me with a cocked eyebrow. "Sasha, get your things."

A warning growl only I can hear emanates from deep in his chest. His Alpha command hits me full force. I spin on my heel and march to Vera. She grabs my arm, and we hurry to her office.

"Oh, Sasha! Do you think he'll keep you from coming back? He's pretty angry."

I shake my head as frustrated tears blur my vision. How could Dylan embarrass me like that? Everyone will think I don't have a mind of my own! I understand his concern for my safety. But he didn't have to shut me down without me even having a say in the matter.

We spoke about the dangers some of the human females face that can follow them to the shelter. And he agreed I could volunteer with the new security system. Sure, a gun adds another element. But unless the bullet is silver, it can't kill me.

I have so many plans to help the residents. Make a difference in the lives of those who need it most. I can't help the she-wolves and human females turned wolf shifters. But I can help the women here. It's not right!

Vera senses my distress and rubs my arm. She doesn't speak, but her presence comforts me. It's best because I'd burst into tears if I opened my mouth.

I get my coat and handbag and give her a hug. She walks with me back to the reception area.

The director still talks to Dylan. But his face is as rigid

as stone. His eyes find mine. But I stare at his chest. I can't bear to look at him. The director makes one last plea. Dylan shakes his head and takes my elbow. The director calls after us, and I wave my hand, too distraught to speak.

Dylan guides me to his motorcycle and puts the new helmet on my head. He bends his knees to align our eyes, but I avert mine. He grumbles and straddles the bike. I don't take his hand. Instead, I grip the seat and swing my leg over. I'm not fool enough to not hold him for the ride. But I don't squeeze him as I normally do. He starts the ignition, and we merge with the traffic.

I hop off the bike as soon as he pulls into the parking space in the garage. He reaches for my arm. But I sidestep and rush towards the exit.

"Sasha! Where are you going?"

I ignore him and break into a sprint. Then a big body slams into me from behind. I pitch forward and brace my hands against a steel post to regain my balance.

"Sasha. Do. Not. Run. From. Me. Ever."

I snarl as his arms bind around me, locking my arms to my sides. His front presses into my back. I struggle to get away. Angry tears threaten to fall, and I don't want him to see.

"Where are you going?"

My mouth remains shut.

He growls in my ear.

"If you're pissed about the shelter, well, too bad. What if you were there that day? He could have hurt you." When I don't respond, he continues. "Enough of this. We're going upstairs."

He turns with me still in front of him. I grind my feet into the ground and refuse to budge.

"I need space."

Dylan freezes.

"I can't be around you right now, Dylan. Let me go. I'll be back in a while."

Shock followed by fear, then anger surge through our mate bond. My breath catches as his emotions wash over me.

"*You can't be around me?!?!?!*" Dylan snarls as he spins me around.

His eyes spark golden fire. A flicker of his angry wolf rises from their depths. The muscles and bones of his face contort as he struggles to hold his shift back.

Now, I see *The Beast* his former pack taunted him as. And it frightens me. For the first time since we met, I tremble with fear of what he's capable of doing to me. My heartbeat speeds up as adrenaline floods my body. I go into flight or fight mode. But if I run now, the deadly predator would chase me down and do who knows what.

His hot breath blows across my face. The tips of his canines appear through his open mouth as he pants. His wolf stares at me.

I lower my eyes in submission and remain still. In no way do I want to provoke him. Not when he's on the edge. He could regain control or plunge into the abyss. I gasp as his claws lengthen and dig into my arms through my cashmere coat. His wolf is winning.

Dylan growls and yanks away forcefully. He swings his head back and forth, then sprints towards his motorcycle. He jumps on and slams the ignition button. The engine roars, and his wolf joins in. The feral cry reverberates around the garage.

The hairs on the back of my neck rise. I clutch my chest as pain and anger strike me through our mate bond. Tears pour from my eyes as I cry out. When he zooms towards me, I raise my hand to him. I don't want him to leave like this, not almost a wild wolf.

He ignores me and flies by straight into the night.

I sag to the ground and throw my head back in a sorrowful howl.

CHAPTER 14

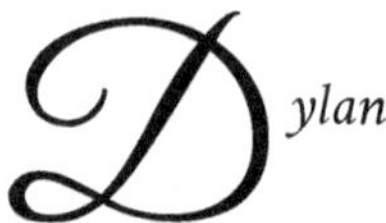 *ylan*

"GLAD YOU'RE BACK. The crowd's been demanding your presence. The other fighters are good, but they don't compare to the draw you have. Tonight's lineup..."

Bennett jabbers on. I ignore him completely.

Shit is fucked up.

I pace the room, trying to hold my wolf in check. Even after hours of riding my Harley to clear my head, I can't get a full grip on my wolf. The only way to settle his anger is to do what I do best. Use my brawn and fight. Release *The Beast*.

Whatever the "lineup," I feel sorry for the human male I face tonight. I won't shift. But I won't hold back my enhanced strength. I'll use just enough to relieve the tension riding me hard—not enough to kill a man. The medical crew better be ready.

I bite back a growl as I relive the scene with Sasha.

How the hell did she expect me to react to some fucker showing up at the shelter with a *gun?*

Should I have laughed it off? Or maybe she wanted me to pat him on the back for a job well done? For scaring the shit out of the human female and the others? What would have happened if Sasha had been there? She always wants to help people. Undoubtedly, she would have tried to stop him. Then what???

My fists clench, and I front kick the table. It flies across the room. The wood splinters on impact with the far wall.

"Hey! Easy now, Vang. I know it's been a while, but don't go all buck wild on me. You need to focus—"

I whirl on him and grab his fancy shirt collar.

"Back the fuck off, Bennett," I warn. "In fact, it's best you go."

I shove him towards the door. One look at my face, and he hightails it out of the room without a backwards glance. I throw my head back for a savage roar. Silence descends in the hallway outside the door. I don't give a fuck.

My chest constricts.

Each time my emotions escalate, they shoot through the mate bond to Sasha. It ricochets with her pain-filled reaction. And it adds to my anger. I'm hurting her even more than when I stopped her from leaving the garage.

"I need space."

"I can't be around you right now, Dylan. I have my mobile and watch. So, I'm safe. Let me go. I'll be back in a while."

Agony sucked the breath from my lungs. I couldn't believe my fated mate wanted nothing to do with me. She'd rather be alone than to spend another second in my presence. Years of pack members avoiding me flashed across my mind. I could take their dislike. But my fated mate?

It took my wolf back to the times he had to protect me from the torment of others. He surged to the surface to start the shift. My entire body reshaped itself—the bones in my face stretched, my spine bent, fingernails grew to claws.

But it wasn't males from my pack fucking with me. It was Sasha—my fated mate—who was upset about her volunteer work. I had to force him down. But not fast enough.

My eyelids squeeze shut to block the image of her stricken face as I held her in my arms and my claws pricked her skin. Dove gray eyes darkened by pupils blown by her fright of *The Beast* she finally witnessed. She didn't move a muscle for fear I would attack. Her breathing even paused.

Now, she knows why they call me *The Beast*.

I had no choice but to get out of there, and fast. Had I stayed longer, I would have shifted. No human can see us as wolves. I raced to my bike and sped off, needing to put distance between my wolf and the source of his frustration. Even her hand held out couldn't stop me. I was too far gone. The only thing to help me is to fight.

A knock at the door jerks me from my thoughts. My escort pokes her head inside. Her timid eyes meet mine. I growl and crack my neck. Here we go!

I stalk out of the room and follow the escort, who hurries ahead of me through the crowd gathered in the hallway. They whisper and point, remembering my roar. Then chants of *The Beast* begin. They don't care a wild and lethal predator lurks amongst them. They live for the savagery of the underground fights.

Keeping my gaze straight ahead, I ignore them until a male slaps me on the back as I pass. With a hiss, I round on him. His back slams into the wall. Plaster crumbles onto his expensive suit jacket. His blue eyes widen. I smell the fear on him and curl my lip. A snarl makes him tremble.

The acrid odor of piss fills my nostrils.

I wrinkle my nose in disgust and loosen my grip on his throat. He drops to the floor. I step over him. Dumb fuck.

The crowd doesn't even care. Their chants increase and they follow me as I walk into the main room. It erupts. Feet stomp the temporary stands. Wolf whistles and barks rise to the ceiling. Females throw their thongs at me. On some of the skimpy bits of silk, I spot phone numbers.

Bennett wasn't lying.

I prowl forward, focused on the cage. At the door, he eyes me warily. I slap him on the chest and nod. He breathes a sigh of relief and opens the door. I duck inside.

The crowd roars.

The announcer tries to speak. Even the mic can't beat the crowd. He waves his hands. Once the volume settles to a steady hum, he speaks. I ignore him, too, and glare at my opponent.

He returns my glare and swoops his arms into a circle in front of his torso. Fists press together. Biceps and triceps flex. He growls.

I roll my eyes.

Enough with the bullshit. Let's get going!

The ref calls us forward and goes over the rules. Anything goes except for action to the heads and the balls.

"Fuck you, *Beast*! I'm ready for you."

Famous last words.

Ten minutes later, the medics carry him from the cage.

Next…

The rest of the fights end the same. I put the opponents down so fast, I go through the lineup in just over an hour. The crowd demands more. And I agree.

Bennett knocks and enters the room.

"Listen, a few guys stepped forward to fight. They're not regulars. But they're fit. Mean as fuck looking. Do you want to get in the cage again?"

I nod. Why not? My wolf needs more time.

Bennett leads the way.

The moment we enter the main room, my wolf snarls and bares his fangs. Golden eyes flash as his hackles rise.

Wolf shifters!

What the fuck!

Garrett must know I'm here and sends me a message.

Well, I'll send them back to him with one of my own. Do. Not. Fuck. With. Me.

I scan the crowd and spot two outside the cage in t-shirts and jeans and one inside stripped to his boxers. The fuckers didn't even come prepared. No matter. They won't last long against *The Beast*.

I stalk forward, keeping the pair by the cage door pinned with a glare. They snicker to each other. One grabs his crotch and jeers at me. My claws itch to lengthen. We may break the rules tonight.

When I approach the cage door, they block my path.

"Save it for the fight, boys."

Unaware of the danger, Bennett steps between three powerful male wolf shifters. He flicks his hand at the pair to shoo them away. They're so shocked by his ballsy behavior, they stare at each other. He reaches past them and unlatches the door, pushing one of them out of the way. He growls.

I throw the fucker a death glare.

He shrugs and guffaws. The other wolf shifter joins in. They step aside with a sweep of their massive arms.

I duck inside, and Bennett shuts the door, then stands by the judges' table.

Boxer Shorts growls.

The announcer speaks, and the ref goes over the rules. He eyes the new fighter. And asks if he understands. The shifter nods.

Then we're on each other.

He's shorter than me by a few inches, but stocky. The shifter is not an MMA fighter. He throws punches and jabs with no kicks or holds.

The first round ends. I release him from the rear-naked choke and rise. He sputters, then leaps up and comes at me, claws lengthened. The ref shouts for him to back down, but the shifter ignores him.

I move with supernatural speed past the shifter and catch him with a back kick. He tumbles forward to land face down on the mat. I pounce and deliver a barrage of punches to his back and flanks, aiming for the delicate organs.

The ref tries to stop me, but I continue until the wolf shifter sags. Our healing ability while fix him in moments. So, I deliver another flurry of punches while his body jerks with each strike. Then I stand and watch him as I back up to the side of the cage.

He caught me with a few jabs. I feel my body repairing itself while I cast a glance at the two outside the cage. With their fingers wrapped around the wires, they glare at me. I flick my gaze to Boxer Shorts. He staggers to his feet and spits blood.

Good.

The ref asks if he wants to continue. He growls and charges me. I repeat the same moves, and he falls again. Dumb fuck.

The fight continues to the final round. The judges declare me the winner.

I glance at the two outside the cage, and as I expected, they charge through the door.

Hell breaks loose.

The ref tries to stop them. One pushes him to the ground and steps on his hand as he passes. The ref screams in pain as his bones crack beneath the wolf shifter's weight. Over the mic, the announcer yells for everyone to leave the cage. The crowd's bloodthirsty shouts for the fight to continue swallow up his demand.

The two flank Boxer Shorts. As one, they roar and race towards me. Their feral wolves shine in their eyes. Faces contort with the shift near. Claws appear.

I'm surprised Garrett allows them to display any part of their wolves. I set the thought aside and prepare for battle.

"Come on!"

SASHA

"MISS? ARE YOU OKAY, MISS?"

I lift my head to find a human male crouching in front of me. His hand rests on my shoulder as he taps me gently. Relief floods his face when I stare at him, then he frowns at the sight of my tear-stained face.

"Do you want me to call someone for you?" He asks as he pulls out his mobile.

I laugh bitterly.

Who would I call?

No family. No pack.

The one I should be able to trust and rely on abandoned me. My fated mate was ready to rip me to shreds! I shudder at the memory of his angry wolf as it contorted Dylan's handsome face. I wrap my arms around myself protectively.

And I don't want to talk to Vera right now. I'm still too upset.

I shake my head and offer the male a wan smile.

"No. But thank you."

"Here, I'll help you up," he says as he holds his hand out. I take it, and he pulls me to my feet. "I can walk you to the elevator if you like."

"No, I'm fine, thank you."

He nods and walks toward the garage's exit. I watch him step into the night, then decide it's a good time to get some fresh air. A run in the park will clear my head, even if I can't shift.

I dab my face with a tissue from the pouch in my handbag. My fingers skim through my hair to ensure it still covers my cheek. I ride the elevator to our penthouse and head to the bedroom, where I change into a long-sleeve t-shirt, running tights, and sneakers.

After I hang up my clothes and put away my handbag, I check my mobile for a missed call or a text message from Dylan. Nothing. Fine. I put my mobile on silent mode and leave it on the center island. I won't take it with me. If I do and he calls, he'll hear I'm outside and lose his shit. When I get back, I'll call. I've had enough arguing for one day.

Instead of taking the elevator to the lobby, I go to the

garage. Perhaps he's back, and we can talk. But the parking space sits empty. Tears prick my eyes. Air! I rush to the exit.

When I step onto Central Park South, I scan the area. I know Dylan will be upset I left the building without him. So, I want to be sure there's no danger. Sensing none, I head for the corner and wait for the light to change.

The sun set a while ago. But the streetlamps provide enough coverage, and my enhanced vision makes it as clear as broad daylight.

I enter the park and head towards the path we usually take. I follow it north towards the zoo. A few joggers pass me as I meander along.

My thoughts replay the scenes with Dylan. I realize he's scared to lose me. He's like me with no one. At least, not here since his mother is still alive and in Miami. But being banished by his pack and the distance make it tough for them.

The pungent smell of grizzly bears indicates I'm near the zoo. The sounds of their huffing carries on the wind as it blows towards me. I wrinkle my nose and hurry on.

A jogger bumps into me from behind.

I spin around to give them a piece of my mind, only to find two males dressed in all black towering over me. They stare with cold, calculating eyes. The hairs on the back of my neck rise.

No! It can't be!

As I call forth my wolf to escape, one of them lunges

towards me. I spot a needle in his hand and raise my arm to deflect it.

Too late.

The pointed tip plunges into the side of my neck. For a second, I think to send a call to Dylan through our mate bond. But darkness overwhelms me. I collapse into the other man's outstretched arms.

ylan

BLOOD SOAKS MY FACE, chest, and arms.

And the cage mat.

It gushes from one wolf shifter's shredded throat to pool around his head. Each pump of his heart forces blood from his body. His buddies were too busy fighting me to notice his leg fading. They could've saved him. Had they covered the wound, he could've healed in time. Instead, Sightless eyes point in my direction.

Boxer Shorts sits on his ass with his back against the cage wire. Blood seeps past his fingers as a hand presses against the gaping wounds in his torso.

The last one peers at me warily as his gaze flicks

between me and his partners. He issues a low growl at me, then turns to lift the dead shifter onto his shoulder. The other staggers to his feet and lurches after him. Before he ducks beneath the cage door, he throws a smirk at me. I flip him the bird.

They push past the silent spectators as the pair head to the exit.

Bennett rushes into the cage, casting a quick glance over his shoulder. He grabs my arm and raises it high. Immediately, the crowd bursts into gleeful shouts. *The Beast. The Beast. The Beast.* Sick fucks.

I shrug out of Bennett's hold and amble towards the cage door. My body needs to recover. *I* need my fated mate.

Now, with the battle over, my mind drifts to her. It must be well past midnight. I picture her curled on her side in the middle of our king-size bed. Ash blonde hair fans out on her pillow. The soft snores she makes whistle past her parted lips.

I can almost taste her sweetness.

Despite the pain racing along my limbs, my cock hardens in the protective cup. I reach into my compression shorts and pull the restrictive piece out. Then roll my eyes when female humans notice and catcall me. They shout offers to take care of my junk. No thanks. My fated mate waits for me in our home.

I'll apologize and make love to her for hours. As I stride into my room, I hear her throaty moans as she cums on my cock for me. Her alabaster skin flushes crimson with her arousal. The tantalizing honey aroma mixes with the Finnish woods and spices of her unique scent. Fuck!

"Who the hell were those guys? Do you know them or something? Because they sure as hell had a vendetta against you. And how the hell did you beat them all? One seemed dead. I started to shoot them with my goddamn gun!"

Bennett rants in the middle of the room with his hands on his hips. He's pissed. I don't doubt he'd shoot them. Too bad regular bullets wouldn't kill them. But I appreciate his loyalty.

"Basic instinct," I respond as I step into the makeshift shower.

I can't show up with blood and gore all over me. My baby would think I freak out. It's bad enough I have to tell her I killed a wolf shifter..

But I do plan to pay Garrett a visit for this bullshit. Why would he risk humans learning about us to prove some point about me being in his territory uninvited? That's a dumb move for an Alpha. He'll tell me something, or I'll challenge his ass. And this time, I won't lose.

I step out of the shower with a towel slung around my hips and one drying my hair.

"So, are you back now or what?" Bennett asks as he leans against the table.

"Yeah. But not tomorrow. A couple of days is good."

"Shit, take a week. You'll need to recover from that

farce of a fight," he says, then frowns. "Damn, I would have thought you'd have more cuts and bruises. You don't even look like you've been in a fight—"

"Listen, I have to get dressed," I cut him off, not wanting him to think too much about my fast healing. "Text the details for a fight in a few days when you have them."

"Sure thing. I'll collect your winnings and bring—"

"Hold them until next time. I gotta go," I say as I move him out the door.

Once he's gone, I toss the towels aside and dress. I ignore the spectators still hanging around, especially the females who rub anywhere on my body they can touch as I pass with my Harley. Their offers for me to ride them instead go unanswered.

Finally outside, I pause and take a deep breath. The cool air invigorates me as it enters my lungs. I stare up at the night sky—inky black, not a star in sight. A few people nod at me and extend congratulatory remarks as I start up my bike. I nod and zoom away.

I take the West Side Highway to the exit on Fifty-seventh Street and ride up Twelfth Avenue to Fifty-ninth before I cross east to our building on Central Park South. I pull into the garage and park, then hop off and jog to our private elevator. The adrenaline pumps through my system.

I can't wait to roll Sasha beneath me. She'll wake with my cock deep inside her tight pussy and cum screaming my name. A carnal grin spreads across my face. I rush through the double doors and jog to our bedroom.

It's quiet, as expected. I don't bother to turn on a light since my wolf vision allows me to see in the dark clearly. So, I'm surprised to find our bed empty—the bedding untouched.

I frown and stride to the bathroom, although I don't hear any sound from inside. Empty. Sasha wasn't in the sitting room when I passed through it.

My heart skips a beat.

"Sasha!" I shout as I run back into the hallway. I continue to call her name as I throw open doors to the other three bedrooms. Nothing. "Sasha! Where are you?"

I race to her studio, praying she fell asleep on the couch inside. It's empty.

My mobile shakes in my hand as I unlock it and pull up the phone app. Her number rings to voicemail. Her sweet voice asking the caller to leave a message punches me in the gut.

Where the fuck is my fated mate?!

Then I remember to channel into our bond. I reach out to her, but no response. Absolute silence. I think back to the last time I felt a connection with her. It was as I zipped through the streets. Maybe forty minutes after I left the garage? I was so in my head I didn't pay attention.

Fuck!

I call down to the concierge.

"Good evening, Mr.—"

"Have you seen my mate... um wife?"

"No, sir. However, I just arrived on shift. Hold one

moment while I check with my predecessor and the doormen."

The wait seems endless. Finally, the concierge returns to the line. "No one has seen Mrs. Vang. Would you like a call should we see her.?"

I grunt a yes and end the call.

Did Sasha leave me? What she promised she'd never do? All because of the shelter?

An ache grows in my chest. The mournful howl of my wolf fills my ears.

I try her mobile again. Voicemail.

Where the hell could she go? It's almost one in the morning?

The shelter!

I whip out my mobile and find the number in my contacts, then call. A sleepy voice answers.

"This is Dylan Vang. Can someone tell me if Sasha is there?"

"Sir, we are not allowed to deny or confirm anyone's presence—"

"She's not a resident!" I bellow. "She's a volunteer! Where's Vera?"

"Sir, please do not raise your voice—"

"Miss, if you do not tell me if Sasha Vang is there or connect me to Vera, I will—"

I stare at the mobile. She hung up. With a growl, I call again. It goes straight to voicemail.

"FUCK!!!"

Sasha must be there. Otherwise, the woman wouldn't insist she can't tell me.

I run to the elevator. In the garage, I hop on my Harley. It roars to life, and I throw my head back and roar with it. Then zoom out of the garage. I make it to the Lower East-side in less than thirty minutes. On the sidewalk, I sniff the air. No trace of Sasha. I take the steps three at a time and jab the intercom.

The same woman answers.

"Is Sasha in there?!"

"Sir, leave the premises, or you will force me to call the police."

My head explodes. My wolf claws under my skin to break free.

"I'm Dylan Vang! The one who just paid thirty-thousand dollars to install this intercom you're speaking on and the rest of the new security system. Tell me if Sasha is in there or get me Vera. Now!"

Silence.

A vision of the ex-husband flashes through my mind. Dammit!

My mobile vibrates in my jeans pocket. Sasha!

"Baby! Where are you?"

"Dylan, it's Vera. What's going on?"

I damn near cry. I thought it was my fated mate. The ache in my chest pulsates.

"Vera... I—I can't find her. She's not at home..."

"You didn't hurt her, did you?"

I growl and bark, "No! Of course not! I left for a fight. She wasn't home when I got back."

"Okay. Hold on, I'll have you buzzed in. I'm not at the shelter, but I'm on my way. I'll be there in twenty minutes."

She ends the call. A moment later, the door buzzes, and I yank it open. A human female in her early twenties glances at me.

"Sorry, Mr. Vang. It's just that so many of us have men in our lives who hurt us. The shelter gives us safety. A place where they can't get us... hurt us. I didn't know who you were until you mentioned the new system. Thank you, by the way. Everyone feels so much better with the improved security. One less thing to worry about."

By the time she's finished, I realize I made a mistake forbidding Sasha from volunteering here. Theses females need people in their lives who care for them and who want to help. I swear, once my fated mate is back in my arms, I'll beg her for forgiveness.

"I'm sorry too. I hope I didn't scare you."

She shrugs but won't meet my gaze. Yeah, I did. Dumbass.

"Forgive me. I have no excuse."

She gives me a little smile and tells me I can wait for Vera in the reception area. Then goes into the receptionist's room behind the security partition and picks up a book.

I can't sit. So, I pace until the sound of someone walking up the front steps reaches my ears. I sniff the air in hopes it's Sasha. No, it's Vera. Dammit!

"Oh, Dylan! I tried calling her too. But it goes straight to voicemail. What happened after you left? Where did you go? Where did you and Sasha separate?"

My heart sinks. If she didn't answer her best friend, where the hell is she? Unless the battery died in her iPhone. I always have to remind her to plug it in. But that still doesn't explain where she is. I answer Vera's questions.

"Okay, she's not with you, here, or with me. The apartment she shared! I'll call over there now."

I pray to the gods Sasha left to stay with her old roommates. That would make sense. Then the bit of hope dies. From Vera's end of the conversation, I can tell the roommates haven't seen or heard from Sasha.

Vera sighs and nibbles her lower lip. Then she snaps her fingers.

"The diner! Maybe she went there since it's open twenty-four hours."

Again, her call ends with a no.

That's it. All the places Sasha knows.

She left me.

I slump onto the wooden bench and drop my head in my hands. My chest burns with the loss of my fated mate. My breathing is shallow.

"Dylan."

Vera's concerned voice slips past the fog. She places a tiny hand on my shoulder. I glance up.

"I know it's hard to do. But try not to worry. Perhaps Sasha checked into a hotel. She said she needed space."

Vera smiles a little and adds, "That's where I would go.

Hunker down with a fudge sundae and fresh-baked chocolate chip cookies from room service and binge watch romcoms. Laugh and not cry about the situation. You should go home and get some sleep. You don't look too good. I'm going to stay here just in case she comes by or calls. I promise to let you know if I hear from her. If no communication in twenty-four hours, we'll go to the police and file a missing person's report. But prayerfully, it doesn't come to that. Okay?"

What Vera says makes sense. It just hurts so bad I can't think clearly. Losing a fated mate can kill the male. And I feel like I'm dying.

I nod and rise, then stumble.

Little Vera catches my arm as though she can hold my big ass up. If I wasn't in such pain, I'd laugh.

"Whoa, there, big boy! You can't ride your motorcycle home. I'll help you bring it in here. You can take a cab."

She's right. I'll kill myself if I ride my bike in this state. She comes with me outside and walks with me as I guide the Harley from the curb, up the stairs, and into the reception room. Then she waits at the top of the stairs until I get in a cab. She waves as the cab pulls off.

I lean back against the seat and think Sasha has a good friend in Vera.

By the time the cab pulls up in front of our building, my head pounds. But I stop by the concierge to ask if Sasha came home. No.

The penthouse seems so empty without her.

I drag myself to the living room and crash on the sofa.

From here, I can see the front door and know the second she comes home. I take off my leather jacket. Before I toss it on a chair, I remove my mobile. I put it within arm's reach on the coffee table and plug it into the hidden charger. I check the ringer is on high, then toe off my boots and stretch out.

Sleep evades me. I flip from one side to the other. Eventually the sun rises. I stand in front of the wall windows and watch Manhattan light up. Somewhere out there, my fated mate wakes. My only hope is she's safe.

Sasha

"Kirill is going to be pleased we brought home his prize."

"I don't know about that since she stinks of another male wolf shifter. Look at his mark on her neck."

"Yeah, well, our brothers must have ended him by now. I wish I could have seen the look on his face when they walked into the cage to fight him. *The Beast,* bah!"

"Don't call them. No communication between our teams."

As I come to, my head pounds. It feels as though I swallowed sand. I try not to make a noise as the Russian wolf shifters speak amongst themselves. But when I open my eyes to see how many of them surround me, the pain is too intense. I cry out. They stop talking.

"Ah, the stupid bitch woke up."

"Not for long."

A shadow looms over me. My arms feel like lead. I can't lift them to protect myself. A sharp jab in my neck, and darkness envelopes me.

My last thought is of my beloved fated mate. Be alive, Dylan.

CHAPTER 16

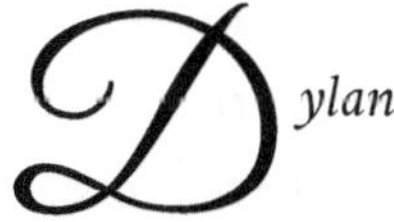

*D*ylan

"SASHA?!"

"N—No, sorry, Dylan. It's Vera. I wanted to ask if you she came home yet. But I guess not."

With a pained groan, I sag back against the wall and throw my arm over my face. I must've fallen asleep. The last thing I remember is pacing in front of the elevator, willing the doors to open and for Sasha to step out.

"What time is it?" I rasp as I pull the mobile from my ear to glance at the screen.

"Six-thirty. I realize it's early. I just couldn't wait. Not to scare you or anything. I called the hospitals to check if a woman matching Sasha's description arrived in the emer-

157

gency rooms. It's routine for us to do at the shelter. Fortunately, she's not at any of them. And trust me, I called them all. I couldn't sleep."

Damn! Why didn't I think of it? Yeah, brawn, not brains.

Vera is a good friend. I thank her. We promise to call as soon as we hear anything. Otherwise, I'll file a missing person's report.

But I won't need the police. I know exactly where to go.

As I rise, the dull ache in my chest throbs. My wolf whines. I rub the spot over my heart and place my palm on the plaque to unlock the double doors to our penthouse.

The emptiness of the massive space bears down on me. In the short time Sasha's been here, she's made her presence known. Her unique scent floats through the rooms. The sweetness of her giggles as I tickle her breathless. Soft hums of Russian melodies as she cooks dinner for us.

Now, nothing besides traces and memories.

After a quick shower, I throw on a hoodie and joggers, then lace up high-top sneakers. I'll grab my motorcycle jacket from the living room chair on my way out.

As I leave my dressing room, I glance at Sasha's. I just need a whiff of her scent. Enough to calm my wolf. Inside, I bring the sleeves of blouses to my nose and close my eyes as I inhale deeply. My heart aches. I turn in a circle to gather her around me. Then I spot her iPhone on the center island.

What the fuck?!

I grab it. The screen shows missed calls and text message alerts from Vera and me. It's on silent mode. No wonder I didn't hear it ringing. I put it in my pocket.

Then I notice her running shoes are missing. Don't fucking tell me she went to Central Park. And. Hasn't. Come. Back!

My heart races faster than my feet as I run through the penthouse to the elevator. As it descends, all sorts of disasters race through my mind. I can't focus on them, or I'll lose my shit before I can find her.

For hours I search the park, going to the different spots we ran to before I check areas thick with trees in case they pulled her beneath them. I go from one end to the other and across. People dodge out of my way as I scream her name. No sign of Sasha.

I leave the park and flag a cab. I check the address on my mobile and tell it to the driver.

As he moves through traffic, he peers at me through the rearview mirror. I recognize I must look like a madman with my hair sticking out all over the place from me yanking it and dirt smudged on my cheeks. Like I give a fuck. When I growl, his eyes skitter to the street ahead.

I use my iPhone to pay and jump out to the sidewalk, then march through the front doors of the office building. Metal and glass swing turnstiles separate the lobby from the rows of elevators. I hop over the turnstiles and jog to the elevators.

"Hey! Hey, you! Stop!"

From all angles, burly security guards rush towards me. I growl and take a fighting stance. Claws out and fangs lengthened. They know what I am, and I know what they are. Their approach slows as they eye me warily. I snarl.

"Take me to Moen. Now!"

They glance at each other. The leader speaks into a mouthpiece as he watches me. I hear him tell someone about me. A pause, then he nods. He narrows his eyes on me and curls his lip to reveal his fangs.

I snort.

"*Mr.* Moen will see you. But if you pull any shit, I will finish you. Come on," he says and heads for an elevator separate from the rest.

The other wolf shifter guards line up for me to pass between them, then close ranks behind me. I glare at each one, daring them to lay a hand on me. The ride up, I brace myself in case they want to try something. They watch me without a word. The doors open, and the leader strides ahead, not threatened by my wild appearance. I follow.

I study my surroundings as we walk. We pass through a reception area with two she-wolves behind a large desk. They gape at me. The leader turns down a hallway lined with glass-front offices. The scents of wolf shifters mix with humans. Only the shifters lift their heads, detecting my wolf as I stalk by.

Ahead of us, a she-wolf rises from her desk to open the double glass doors. Beyond them, Garrett Moen sits behind a desk. His eyes meet my glare unblinkingly. An enormous wolf shifter stands beside him, arms crossed over a broad chest. His lip curls.

I sneer.

"I'm telling you, Vang, do not fuck with me."

My eyes narrow as I stare back at the leader. How the fuck does he know my name? I expected Moen to know and probably his beta—who must be the guy next to him. But this shifter?

The she-wolf eyes me as I enter the office. I ignore her.

"Where the fuck is she, Moen?" I seethe between my teeth.

His beta steps forward as the guards form a protective circle around me.

"You dare come in here and question our Alpha, Vang?!"

I flick my gaze to the beta and snarl.

"Fuck yes. He took my fated mate," I growl, then shift my gaze back to Moen. "And I want her back. Now!"

Moen frowns and shakes his head as he stands.

"What the hell are you talking about? I didn't take your fated mate, Vang. I know you have a she-wolf living with you. But I don't have her."

He tells his guards and beta to stand down.

"How do you know I have a she-wolf and where I live?!"

Moen snorts and folds his arms over his muscular chest as he leans against the side of his desk.

"You think you can come into my territory, in my back-yard, and I don't know it? The fuck you take me for, Vang? I am Alpha of the New York Wolves Pack. Nothing happens without my knowledge—here or in the rest of my territory."

He crosses his long legs at the ankles—letting me know he has no fear of me—and cocks his head.

"Oh, and the underground fight club? I own it."

A chuckle falls from his lips at my surprised expression. I replace it with a scowl and cross my arms over my chest, mimicking his stance of nonchalance.

"Yeah. I figured it's the best way to keep you and your *beast* under control. Not a move you made went unwatched. You disrespected me by not seeking my permission to stay within my territory. But I let it go. Best to keep a rogue wolf in plain sight."

"Listen, I'm not here to listen to your rambling, Moen. I'm—"

"Sorry, Alpha. I had to—"

A trace of the woody and spicy aroma of the Finnish forests fills my nostrils. I whirl around to face the door.

Not Sasha.

A giant of a wolf shifter stands there. For a second, his eyes widen at the sight of me. Then he blanks his face. But he can't hide the uptick of his heartbeat or the beads of sweat at his hairline. This fucker knows where Sasha is!

With a savage growl, I knock two guards out of the way and lunge at him. Claws extend and fangs lengthen as a red haze descends before my eyes.

He raises his fists with a snarl.

We crash. Claws rake through his suit jacket and into his flesh. He gets in a punch to my flank. But I knock his head against the doors. The glass doesn't break, but he bellows in pain. I grip his throat as my arm draws back, first ready to break his face.

"ENOUGH!!!"

Powerful hands grab me. I roar and kick the shifter in the chin. Four guards drag me away as I snarl and flail. The others grab the giant and haul him to his feet. He snarls and jerks to free himself. I match his intensity. But the guards maintain their firm grips.

"Where the fuck is she?! What did you do to her?!"

"Fuck you!"

Moen and his beta step between us.

The Alpha cocks his head at the giant.

"Hudson, what did you do?"

His lips flatten into a thin line.

"Hudson. What. Did. You. Do?" Moen's deep menacing growl hits the giant with his irresistible Alpha command.

He lowers his gaze and mutters words under his breath. My wolf enhanced hearing can't catch them.

"LOUDER!!!"

The giant visibly trembles in the wake of Moen's command. He lifts his head and glares at me.

"When I was surveilling Vang, I saw the bitch with him at a fight and recognized her from the photos sent to the network."

The guards tighten their grip on me when I lunge forward, snarling.

"I'll rip your fucking heart out of your chest with my bare hand!"

Moen swings his gaze to me. His arctic blue eyes blaze with anger.

"I will handle this, Vang," he bites out, then returns his attention to the giant. "You better tell me everything from start to finish, or *I* will rip you apart piece by fucking piece."

The giant's eyes flit across Moen's face. What he sees has him spilling his guts before I do it for him.

It's worse than I feared. I thought Moen took Sasha to get back at me for being in his territory. In that scenario, I could work with easily. But this?

The fucker kidnapped her from Central Park with Russian wolf shifters. The same ones Sasha escaped from. They tranquilized her, which explains the silence over our mate bond. They drove her back to the rural outskirts of Pennsylvania hours ago! She must be there by now.

My mind goes wild with thoughts of what that Russian fucker could do to her. Right. Now. I throw my head back and howl. My wolf joins in my anguished cry.

"Vang."

I open my eyes to stare at Moen.

"We will get your fated mate back. But I need your word you will kill none of the wolf shifters until we know every detail of their operation. My own man crossed me to work for them. This shit is in my territory, and I cannot allow it to continue. From the sounds of it, more than one cell of these Russian wolves exists throughout the country. I'll need to speak with the other five Alphas on the Ruling Council. But first, I gather my enforcers, and we head out, including you. Do I have your word, Vang?"

"Yes, and I will help you get rid of all the fuckers. They cut my fated mate's face with a dull switchblade from temple to jaw, then poured salt in the wound to prevent it from healing. I've thought of thousands of ways to torture them, and I will have my day."

Moen nods, and the guards release me. He strides over to a cabinet and takes out a box and thick leather gloves. He approaches the giant.

"You will come with us. If you do anything to interfere, I will gut you like the pig you are. Take off your jacket and roll up your sleeves," Moen says as he nods for the guards to turn the giant around. "Put your hands behind your back. These shackles are pure silver."

The giant struggles, but the guards hold him fast. He hisses, then howls as the shackles clamp with clicks around his bare wrists. The stench of burning flesh fills the room. Moen removes the giant's tie and uses it as a gag to muffle his pitiful cries.

"Have a seat while I make some calls," Moen says to me as he stalks to his desk. "Meanwhile, do you need anything? Something to eat or drink? I hate to say it, but you look like shit, Vang."

I growl, and he shrugs.

But he's right. The separation from my fated mate compounded with the knowledge she's vulnerable in the hands of those brutes zaps my energy. I need it more than ever to fight them.

"A couple of rare steaks and some water," I say with a snort, not expecting the request to be met.

Surprisingly, Moen nods and turns to his beta.

"Dolph, call the flight crew and tell them about the order. They need to prepare the Sikorsky helicopters. We'll meet them at the West 30th Street Heliport in thirty minutes…"

He goes on to make plans based on the info from the giant and the bits of details Sasha gave me. I admire Moen's efficiency and calmness. It's not long before we pile into Suburbans and head to the heliport. During the ride, we complete the plan of attack. The most important thing for me is getting my fated mate back. Then killing that fucker Kirill Gusev.

By the time we land, the sun set. It's a moonless night with no wind—perfect to invade the Russian pack.

SASHA

"SHE CARRIES the stink of that stupid fighter—*The Beast*! She let him touch her, mark her with his claiming bite?! Sasha Volkov was meant to be mine when she came into heat! Mine! Now, look at her…"

Kirill's shouting wakes me from another drug-induced sleep.

The captors keep me blindfolded and bound with handcuffs lying on my side. My body aches where the numbness in my hands and feet doesn't reach. No moisture fills my eyes or mouth. They're so dry, they scratch and burn. Once I awoke to vomit in my mouth and choked it out. Now, my stomach roils, but nothing comes up. The ache in my head matches my heart.

Dylan! I need my fated mate. I pray to the gods they didn't kill him.

But I can't summon up the energy to use our mate bond. The drugs weaken me. I can't even call my wolf forth to help me. I don't know what they gave me. Her presence is no longer felt on the fringes of my being.

The cold metal beneath me sends chills through the long-sleeve t-shirt and running tights. I shiver, and the metal from the handcuffs clangs on the floor.

Kirill goes quiet. No sound except for his angry breaths. I do not know how many wolf shifters surround me since I only hear his rant.

Heavy boots stomp across the metal floor. It clangs beneath my ear with each step. I bit back a cry as my headache worsens. The sound grows sharper as the boots approach me. A hand yanks the blindfold from my eyes.

I gasp and blink, closing my eyes. Although weak, the overhead light blinds me. My eyes prove too sensitive after hours of being covered.

A calloused hand grabs my chin and jerks my head back.

"You ran away from me a third time, Sasha Volkov. You did not learn from the last lesson. Did you? Perhaps I should add a second cut on your other cheek to match the first one. Or maybe I should remove your eyes with a spoon. Then you won't be able to see to run away again."

Sobs rack my body.

"What a dumb bitch. You mated with another wolf shifter. Bear his mark. Now, you ruined yourself. I no longer want you, Sasha Volkov. But I'll still make some good money off you. An Alpha whose mate died in childbirth is desperate enough to buy you since you're the daughter of an Alpha. He figures you're quality stock. He doesn't care about the hole in your face. Oh, no. He only wants the hole between your legs!"

Kirill laughs like a maniac and slams my head to the metal floor.

An excruciating pain explodes from the blow to my temple in the exact spot at the beginning of the scar. I cry out as my body jerks from the impact. My stomach flips. Bile I didn't realize I had erupts from my mouth to puddle beneath my cheek. I'm too weak to move away from it. The odor makes me vomit again.

"You dirty bitch! Look at you wallowing in your filth!" Kirill snarls. "Get her cleaned up. Her new master will be here in a few hours to take her home."

Tears pour from my eyes to blend into the mess below. I can't believe I'm back with Kirill and he's sold me to some Alpha. My happy life with my fated mate never had a chance to flourish.

Suddenly, I'm yanked upright and shoved against the

metal wall. The back of my head bangs against it, and I cry out.

"Shut your whiny mouth before I put something in it!"

More tears slip past my closed eyelids at the vicious threat.

"And quit your blubbering!"

The disembodied voice wipes a rag over my face.

"Throw up again, and I'll force you to eat it."

I swallow and lower my head. Never have I felt so defeated.

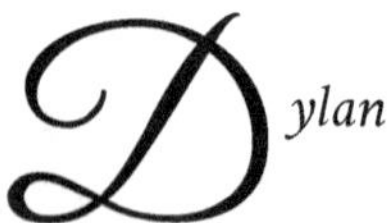ylan

"Remember, my men know what you look like and what you wear. They will not attack you. Any others that confront you are fair game, except for Gusev. I need him alive to learn about his network. Got it?"

"Yeah. Now, let's go!"

We left the helicopters a few miles away from the location Hudson provided. Moen's tech team did surveillance and found his info accurate since several heat signatures mill about the property. Most of them gather in one structure, I guess as the barn. A few others appear in different areas in what must be the house. Ten single ones move along the perimeter. In all, about fifty blips appear on their screen. From what

Hudson tells us, twenty male wolf shifters always remain on site.

Moen's enforcers split into two groups to approach from opposite sides with the property in the middle. Some of them will shift into wolves while the others remain in human form with semi-automatic weapons, handguns, and knives. They're full-on commando. I knew Moen was into some shit. But I had no idea he was such a badass.

I'm no fool. So, I strapped on a holster with two handguns and ammo. Moen gave a run-through on how to use them. A communication piece rests in my ear. I won't shift unless I have to. While Moen and his enforcers go after the Russian pack, my goal is to find Sasha and bring her to the helicopters. I still can't sense her and hope the tranquilizers wear off by the time we get to the site.

We move forward in clusters, keeping low. A thick forest surrounds the site on all sides provides ample coverage. But we're mindful of fallen branches and twigs that can snap beneath our feet. It's so quiet, the wolf shifters would easily hear the sound.

Suddenly, a techie shifter's voice comes over the ear comm.

"Cameras around the perimeter spotted. Hold on while we connect to force them to loop."

I flex my hands, itching to run ahead and search for my fated mate. But I won't risk the operation. We're too close to fuck up. Instead, I send out a call through our mate bond, then wait for a response. Not a damn thing.

Then a thought pops into my mind.

What if she's... *dead?*

I stagger as though shot in the chest with one of Moen's weapons.

He grabs me by the arm.

"What happened? Is it your fated mate?"

I manage to shake my head as I steady myself.

"Good to move forward," the techie announces.

Thank fuck! I don't know how much longer I can wait.

Moen gives me a hard look, and I wave him off. He nods and raises his hand for the signal to move ahead.

As one, the enforcers in wolf and human forms follow their Alpha's lead as though accustomed to missions like this one. My wolf hearing detects a few garbled grunts. The metallic scent of blood wafts to my nostrils. Some of the patrolling Russians get eliminated. As we pass, I see their throats slit from ear to ear and eyes poked out. Good.

Lights from the barn and house appear through the trees as we reach the edge of the forest. I glance beyond to look for the second team. From the distance, I can't make them out in the shadows. But the word comes through they're in position.

Moen, Dolph, and nine of his enforcers step from the coverage provided by the forest and head for the barn. The she-wolves and human females turned shifters will get secured to avoid them becoming casualties of the invasion.

The other ten enforcers race to the house. I go with them since Sasha told me that's where Kirill kept her in a room upstairs with other she-wolves who hadn't gone into heat yet. As we reach the porch steps, gunfire erupts behind the barn.

Fuck!

I charge for the door. It's locked.

"I got it," one enforcer says as he shoots the wood beside the lock. It falls free. He kicks the door open, and crouches, weapon raised.

Shouts in Russian sound from inside. We move in cautiously. A snarl comes from our left, then a massive wolf appears. It snaps its jaws, ears flattened to its head, and hackles raised. It leaps in the air.

POW. POW.

The wolf crashes to the ground, writhing as it howls in agony. Silver-dipped ammo finishes him.

The Russians run from the back. Moen's enforcers engage with them while I dash up the stairs. I sniff the air for Sasha. Not a whiff. But I hear female cries for help down the hallway. I can't leave them.

I race towards the door on the end. Two locks keep it secure.

"We're here to save you! Step away from the door! Do you understand?"

"Yes!"

"Please help us!"

A chorus of cries ring out.

"Go to the other side of the room. Now!"

I hear them shuffle away and shoot the wood, mimicking the enforcer. The wood splinters, and I kick the door in. The stench of body odor and waste assail my nostrils. Damn!

No source of light to illuminate the room exists. My enhanced vision spots stained mattresses on the floor. Empty plates of food and bottles of water sit beside them. Five females in tattered clothing and barefoot huddle in a corner by the window.

"Sasha, have you seen Sasha? Ash blonde hair and dove gray eyes."

They shake their heads no.

Fuck!

A commotion on the stairs draws my attention. I raise my hand to tell them to stay, then crouch to peer around the doorframe. Amber eyes narrow on me. A hulk of a wolf leaps the last few steps and lands at the end of the hallway. A low growl comes from his mouth as he stalks forward.

"Don't come out!" I yell to the females as I step into the hallway.

They whimper and huddle closer together. Terror etched on their gaunt faces.

I aim a gun at the wolf. It leaps in the air as I pull the trigger. And miss.

It snarls in victory as its front paws land on my chest. The impact knocks me on my back. The gun clatters into the room. Claws dig into my chest, past my hoodie. Putrid breath fills my nose. Spit drips onto my face from its sharp fangs inches from my face.

I turn my head to the side. My hands fist its fur while my knees jerk up and ram into its hind legs. It yelps and falls off balance. I backflip to my feet and draw the other gun, aim, and shoot three rounds into its chest. It collapses, howling in pain.

I rush into the bedroom. A she-wolf hands the gun to me. I nod my thanks and tell them to follow me.

"Wait! There's another room with she-wolves across the hall," someone says.

I frown, surprised they have made no noise.

"They're in awful shape. The males put those of us who fight back in there. No food or water for days," she explains. "But be careful. They may attack you since you're a male."

The door across the hall has three locks. I put my ear to the wood. No sound.

"Vang, the house is secure. No sign of Sasha. What's happening up there?"

The ear comm comes to life.

"Five females secured, but more behind a door. Someone come up. I have to find my fated mate."

"Roger that."

I turn to the females and tell them to wait for the enforcers. They thank me as three males rush up the stairs. I race past them and step onto the porch cautiously as I scan the area. Enforcers aim weapons at Russians lying on the ground in front of the barn.

Moen exits the structure and glances in my direction. He waves me over.

"Sasha isn't in there. The females haven't seen her since she escaped—"

"Sasha? Did you say Sasha?"

We spin around to face a Russian on the ground. He stares, eyes flicking between us.

I rush over and yank him to his feet by the scruff of the neck. His eyes widen in fear. But he mouths, not here, and flicks his gaze at the ones on the ground. They watch our every move. I drag him into the barn away from them.

"Speak up, or I'll rip your heart out," I snarl.

"We need information, Vang," Moen warns, then faces the young shifter. "What do you know about Sasha? Where is Kirill?"

"I helped her to escape after he cut her face. I drove her to the bus station and gave her all the money I saved and some clothes," he answers in hushed tones. Fearful eyes dart to the barn door. "But I didn't know she was back."

Then it hits me. He's the one Sasha talked about. The only one whose name she revealed.

"Ivan?" I ask, and he nods. "They kidnapped her from New York City and brought her here. Where can she be? Speak fast. We have little time!"

He thinks a moment, then his eyes widen. "She must be the package an Alpha is picking up."

"WHAT???"

Moen and I shout in unison.

"Hurry! He may be here already! Come with me. I'll take you to the pickup location. But bring your pack and your guns. Kirill is dangerous and tricky."

I growl, and Moen curses as he speaks into the ear comm.

We leave the second team to watch the Russians and females. Ivan leads us through the forest a distance away from the site. Then he pauses and turns to me.

"Kirill doesn't want the buyers to know the location of the barn. So, he meets them here. The building over there is where he keeps the operation's office and computers. That metal structure is where he holds the females until the buyers arrive. It's bulletproof and soundproof accessed by one door with a plate Kirill puts his right palm on to unlock it. He usually has his beta and head enforcer with four soldiers with him. *Blyad'*! The buyer's car approaches. Look there!"

SASHA

"PLEASE. I—I have to go to the bathroom."

The male wolf shifter Kirill left with me glares at my request as he sits on a chair by the door.

"Please. I don't want to wet myself."

He rolls his eyes and lumbers to his feet, then jerks me to my feet. I stagger behind him as he drags me to a corner where an empty bucket sits. He pushes me towards it. My shoulder bumps into the metal wall. Pain zings through me. I bite back a cry, knowing he may hit me.

I don't bother to point out my hands cuffed behind my back and ankles cuffed together will make it difficult for me to do my business. I don't want to give him any ideas. So, I do my best. It's messy. But I have no other choice. When I finish, I slide along the wall away from the bucket, and sag to the floor.

An intercom buzzes. Kirill speaks in Russian to let the male know the buyer arrived.

My heart clenches. Tears stream down my cheeks.

Oh, Dylan! I love you so much! We didn't have enough time together. I'm so sorry, my love. So very sorry.

I throw my head back and howl. The anguished cry reverberates around the metal room. It goes on and on until it morphs into a yelp.

"Shut the fuck up, you dumb bitch!" The male shifter shouts as he backslaps me across the face.

The opposite cheek hits the metal wall. My teeth cut into my lower lip. Blood fills my mouth from the gash. The room spins. I whimper and scoot away from him as best as I can, still bound. My head hangs.

"Better," he grumbles and returns to the chair.

The intercom squawks to life. Kirill shouts for the male to not open the door. They're under attack.

My heart thumps in my chest. I pray to the gods Dylan found me. Then another thought scares me. What if the Alpha who planned to buy me is the attacker? What if he doesn't want to pay and will fight to take me? My stomach churns. Bile rises. I turn my head to the side and vomit.

An eerie silence descends on the room. I risk a glance at the male. He glares at me. I drop my gaze and listen for sounds of a fight. Only the silence. The room must be soundproof. The intercom remains silent. Time stretches on, increasing my distress.

Suddenly, the door slams open. It bangs against the wall.

Ignoring the pounding in my skull, I jerk my head up, wanting to face the dreaded Alpha. I blink when Dylan appears soaked in blood. I close my eyes to make sure I'm not hallucinating, then open them. His golden eyes shine with love as he kneels in front of me.

"*Saaashaaa,*" he breathes as he pulls me into his arms.

I winch from the pinch in my shoulders.

"Oh, fuck, baby! Sorry!" He exclaims as he loosens his hold.

"No, Dylan, hold me!" I sob as I lean forward to press my face into his neck. "Hold me… Hold me… Never let me go…"

My body shakes uncontrollably as sobs rack my body.

"Dylan, we need to move out. Let me remove the cuffs."

I glance up into glacial blue eyes.

The male wolf shifter nods at me. Dylan growls.

"Okay, then you do it. But hurry the fuck up!" The male says and hands a key to Dylan, who hurriedly frees my wrists and ankles.

He scoops me into a bridal hold and runs after the male. When I spot the Russian on the metal floor with a bullet hole between his open, lifeless eyes, I bury my face in Dylan's chest. The amount of blood in the crisp night air lets me know carnage took place outside of the room—or rather metal structure.

Vibrations from Dylan's rumble soothe me as we speed through the forest. I hear other wolf shifters and the soft cries of females.

"Split the females into two helicopters with two enforcers in each and Dylan in one. The Russians with me, Dolph, five enforcers. The rest get in the other helicopters. When we land, we go straight to The Tower. Go! Go!"

Dylan carries me aboard and buckles me in a seat, then drops into one next to me. He reaches over and cups my face.

"I love you, my fated mate. Forever."

I didn't think I could cry anymore and burst into joyful tears. He unbuckles his seatbelt to lean over and kisses me breathless. Then he presses his forehead to mine and sighs before he buckles in.

My eyes scan the females. I recognize a few, and they murmur words of thanks. I nod and let my eyes drift shut. Exhausted with drugs still in my system, my body demands sleep. I give in.

When I awake, I'm in a bed with an IV attached to the back of my hand. A steady beat pulses in the background. Dylan holds my other hand as his head rests on the mattress. I glance around the room. It's all white with a table in the corner and a door leading to a small bathroom. I sniff the air. We're not home.

Dylan stirs, then lifts his head. A smile blooms across his face.

"Hi, baby. How do you feel?"

I scan my body for any aches and find none. I grin and squeeze his hand.

"Great! So much better. Rejuvenated even."

He chuckles.

"The doctor pumped you with fluids to flush your system and to rehydrate you. Your wolf did the rest," he responds, then lowers his eyes. When he lifts them, they're full of concern. "But did they... Um... No one bothered you, did they?"

I shake my head.

"No, not in *that* way. Thank the gods! They kept me drugged up and slapped me around quite a bit," I respond, then run my tongue over the gash on my lip. It's healed.

Dylan's eyes darken to burnished gold as a growl rumbles deep in his chest. He closes them at my touch on his check.

"I'm fine, my love. You saved me from a horrific situation," I say, then lower my voice as I recall the future Kirill planned for me. "Kirill sold me to an Alpha. His mate died in childbirth. So, he wanted me as a breeder since I'm the daughter of an Alpha. 'Quality stock,' as he said."

I shudder at the memory and swallow down bile.

Thankfully, a knock on the door interrupts my train of thought. Dylan calls for them to enter.

An older male wolf shifter with a white coat on and a stethoscope around his neck enters with a nurse she-wolf in a colorful uniform behind him. He beams.

"Hello, Sasha! Good to see you awake. I'm Dr. Carlson, and this is Nurse Horn. How do you feel?"

"Wonderful, Dr. Carlson, thanks to Dylan and you!"

He does a quick check while my fated mate eyes his every move. Then the doctor steps back and studies my face.

I blush and reach to pull my hair over my cheek. Dylan growls and rises.

"What the fuck you staring at?"

Dr. Carlson raises his hands palms out and takes a step back. Nurse Horn gasps.

"Whoa, there, Dylan. I'm not 'staring' as you think. More considering options," the doctor says, then turns to me. "Moen told me about the scar and the salt. I believe I can remove the scar."

Now, I gasp, and Dylan lowers to his chair.

asha

"ARE YOU NERVOUS? You know you don't have to do this. Nothing can diminish your beauty, baby. I love you just as you are."

Dylan strokes my cheek as he stares at me with concern in his eyes.

I close my eyes and nuzzle against his hand.

These last few days prove I need to start fresh. Time to leave the past behind. Restart my life with my fated mate and enjoy every moment of we share.

Dylan told me how he caught my scent on Garrett's head enforcer, and he confessed to kidnapping me. Their rescue plan saved me and the other she-wolves plus the human females turned shifters. Those who have packs to return to left. The others remain with Garrett during their recovery. He'll help them find new homes, or they can stay with his pack.

When Dylan told me Ivan led them to the metal structure, I cried for joy. He was alive and well and helped save me again! I insisted Garrett allowed Ivan to visit me. Garrett gave his permission. Despite Dylan's grumbling, I gave Ivan a big hug. The young wolf's face flushed bright red.

Since he was the omega of his pack in Russia, he ran away. Soon after, Kirill recruited him. Unfortunately, Ivan didn't know the extent of Kirill's heinous activities. By the time Ivan witnessed the atrocities, it was too late. If Ivan tried to leave, Kirill would have killed him. So, Ivan kept his promise and protected the females as best he could. He would sneak food and water to them of offer to guard them to prevent the other males from hurting them.

Now, Garrett gave him the same choice as the females. Ivan said it didn't take him long to pledge his loyalty to the New York Wolves Pack Alpha. He'll work as an enforcer and help to eliminate the rest of Kirill's network.

I told Ivan I would love for him to join Dylan and me for a Russian feast I'd cook to celebrate. He accepted enthusiastically. Dylan nodded and clapped the young wolf shifter on the shoulder.

After he left my hospital room, I asked Dylan about Kirill and the ones who lived.

They only brought back to New York City Kirill, his beta, and two others. They killed the rest. Dylan explained

the blood covered him before he entered the metal structure belonged to Kirill. My fated mate hacked Kirill's hand
off with a machete to use his palm to open the door. Dylan
vowed he'd dismember the rest of Kirill once Garrett
finished interrogating him. The others—along with
Garrett's enforcer—will face the same judgement. I feel
zero sympathy for them. The monsters!

Garrett's cleanup crew razed the buildings and burned
the bodies to ashes. I thank the gods for the end of a reign
of terror.

I spoke with Vera on the phone to assure her I was well.
I told a tiny lie that I had to go out of town for a few days
to clear my head. She sighed in relief, then demanded I
never pull a stunt like that again!

Dylan admitted he overreacted and gave in to me
continuing my volunteer work at the women's shelter. He
even promised to donate funds for the comfy home
makeover.

So, am I nervous? Absolutely not.

"No, my love. I'm excited about our new beginning, and
it starts with this," I respond to my fated mate as I wave my
hand. "I love you more than anything in this world or
thereafter, Dylan Vang."

Tears shine in his golden eyes. He bends over and
brushes his lips over mine. His tongue slips between my
parted lips. It coaxes mine to tangle with it. With a sigh, I
give myself over to his passion.

A polite cough separates us. Dylan grumbles, and I
giggle.

"The doctor is ready for you, Sasha," Nurse Horne says as she steps through the door. "I'll take you to the operating room. Are you ready?"

I glance at Dylan and grin.

"Absolutely!"

He leans over and presses a kiss to the scar.

"My Beauty. Forever."

An hour later, I awake from the surgery. Dylan sits beside the bed, holding my hand. He grins when our eyes meet.

"Dr. Carlson said it went better than expected. He cut around the scar deep enough to remove the dead tissue. Then he cleaned the wound. Your wolf healing took care of the rest," Dylan says and holds up a hand mirror. "Look, a complete success!"

If not for his excitement, I would have been too afraid to look, expecting to find a worse scar than before. But as I peek at the mirror, my breath catches.

Flawless alabaster skin on both cheeks!

I cry out loud with joy. My fingertips touch the fresh skin gingerly. It's smooth as silk. No sign of trauma whatsoever.

"You were gorgeous before and even more so now, baby. Dr. Carlson said if you're up to it, we can go home. He'll come by and check on you once more, then we can leave. How do you feel?"

"Fabulous. Let's go home, my love. I miss you and need you, Dylan," I purr.

His nostrils flare as his wolf flashes in his golden eyes.

He races from the room. A moment later, Dr. Carlson and Nurse Horn enter behind him.

I thank the doctor profusely. Then he clears me to leave.

Dylan hustles them out the door so I can change into the sweater, yoga pants, and sneakers he brought. He refuses to let me walk and carries me from the hospital wing of the New York Wolves Pack's Tower and out the main door to the curb.

The she-wolves we pass giggle and egg us on. I throw my head back and laugh. My waist-long hair cascades down my back, exposing my entire face for the first time in months.

I wave for a cab since Dylan's hands are full. He puts me inside, and I scoot over to give him room. The entire ride home, we kiss like teenagers. The driver taps the partition to tell us we arrived. We laugh as Dylan pays the fare. He hops out and scoops me up. We zip past the doorman and the concierge as we head for our private elevator. We enjoy another ride with heated kisses until Dylan steps out to the entry foyer.

He doesn't hesitate and runs through the penthouse for our bedroom suite. I giggle as a bump along, arms wrapped around his neck. Then yelp as he tosses me to the king-size bed. I bounce, and he pounces.

My fated mate makes passionate love to me for hours. We can't get enough of each other. Brief naps and snacks sustain us until we pass out, too spent to move a muscle. Dylan pulls me close with his chest pressed to my back and a leg thrown over mine. He buries his face in my hair and murmurs how much he loves me. I kiss the biceps where I rest my cheek and fall into a peaceful slumber.

DYLAN

ONCE AGAIN, I sit on the sofa and watch Sasha as she sleeps in our king-size bed after hours of lovemaking. Curled in a ball on her other side, her silky hair fans out on the pillow and down her back. The unblemished skin of her cheek serves as a reminder of her vow to live anew.

And I'm going to give her everything she wants and then some. Starting with the little red box with gold scrollwork in my palm. She bears my mark from my claiming bite, carries my scent beneath her skin, and goes by my name. Now, she will wear my ring for all the world to see Sasha Vang is mine. Mine!

She must sense my emotions through our mate bond. Her head lifts from the pillow and sleepy dove gray eyes peer at me. A soft smile blooms on her gorgeous face.

"What are you doing so far away from me, my love? I miss you already. Come back to bed and hold me close."

I grin and go to my fated mate, then pull her into my arms. I place a kiss on top of her head and lean back.

"You never have to miss me, Sasha Vang. I will be with

you for all eternity," I declare, then hold my palm out to her.

A gasp slips from her lips when I press the gold button closure. A Cartier diamond eternity band nestles in velvet, sparkles like Sasha's dove gray eyes when she laughs with joy. Or shine with tears as they do now.

With a smile, I pluck the eternity band from the box and place it on her left ring finger, then kiss it. I turn her hand over and kiss the other side. I blaze a trail of kisses down her palm, across her wrist, and up her arm to my mark on her neck, then further to her luscious lips.

She moans as her fingers tangle in my hair to pull me closer. Our tongues dance an erotic tango with rhythmic thrusts and sucks set to a backdrop of sensual groans. Her sweet honey arousal tantalizes my wolf senses.

I crave more.

Her thighs spread to welcome me as I press her into the pillows and rock my pelvis against hers. She mewls into my mouth. Her hands lower to grip my ass as her hips roll. The friction goes straight to my hungry cock.

The plum-shaped head slips past the drawstring waist of my black silk pajama bottoms. It thumps in response to the sensuous heat of her bare skin. I groan for more.

Sneaky little fingers slide along my v cuts to pinch the bulbous tip. I groan as pre-cum oozes out of the slit. She smears it across the head, and I growl deep in my chest.

"Ah, My Little Wolf wants to play."

She mewls and slips her fingers down the thick veiny shaft. A fingernail teases the one leading to my cum-filled balls. A zing of desire skates along the vein. I buck in her hand and growl low and husky deep in my chest.

Three fingers delve past her slick, swollen folds. Heat and wetness envelop them. The long middle finger flexes and curls to stroke the sensitive spot on the front wall of her pussy. Once. Twice.

Her back arches from the pillows, lifting her full pillowy tits to my eager mouth as she keens. The orgasm overtakes her. It continues as I suckle hard on her ripe nipples and plunge my fingers in and out, fucking her through the climax. Waves hit her and crest. Her pussy gushes into my palm.

"Cum for me, My Little Wolf. Don't stop. Cum for your fated mate!"

Her pussy clenches on my fingers and sucks them in deeper. My thumb flicks at her engorged clit. Teasing circles drive her hips to undulate. Her body shudders beneath me as I force another orgasm from her pulsating pussy. Her mouth opens in a silent scream.

Swiftly, I flip her onto her belly and grip her hips to pull her ass high.

"Tell me I'm yours! Tell me you belong to me!" I bark as my cock slams into her cunt.

She screams and clenches around my girth.

"Yeesss!"

I plunder her pussy with pistoning strokes.

As I watch my cock stretch her lower lips and disappear balls deep inside of her, a carnal haze fills my vision. I want her belly round with my pup. She will bear my pups. No one else's. MINE!

Everything ceases to exist except for the primal urge to fill her womb with my seed. My fingertips dig into her hips. Held fast, she can only accept the brutal thrusts. My groin slams into her ass with each snap of my hips. Balls slap her clit.

The wet sounds mingle with her throaty moans and my feral grunts. Sex, sweat, and musk mix with woods and spices to fill the air with an enticing aroma. I inhale it deep into my lungs, driven wild by the smell.

I howl as my knot expands at the base of my cock. One last thrust wedges it deep into her spasming pussy. Locking her to me. My fated mate. My pup. MINE!

She screams and fists the sheets as her head thrashes from one side to the other. Sweat dampens her silky ash blonde hair.

I wrap it around a fist and pull to bow her back. My teeth nip the delicate shell of her ear down to the lobe. She yelps.

"Yes. You. Are. All. Mine."

My hips pump to emphasize each word as I lave the pain away. My warm breath blows in her ear.

"*O, bogi! Blyad'!*"

Her pussy contracts and squeezes my dick. I growl from the erotic pain as she milks every last drop of seed from my heavy balls. The flutters of her pussy walls along my length make my legs tremble.

Banding an arm around her waist, I lower us to our

sides. She moans and arches her back. Her round ass nestles against my groin. It feels so good. I close my eyes on a sigh.

"I love you, baby," I say with a raspy voice.

She turns her head to find my lips for a passionate kiss, then breathes, "I love you more, my love."

~

SASHA

"WHAT ARE YOU GOING TO COOK—"

The ring of Dylan's mobile interrupts his question as he sits at the breakfast counter in the chef's kitchen.

"What does Moen want?" Dylan grumbles as he glares at the screen.

You would think he'd be less bristly with the New York Wolves Pack Alpha since they helped to save me and the others. But not my beast of a fated mate!

I stifle a giggle as I close the French doors of the Sub-Zero refrigerator. The ingredients for dinner sit on the counter, ready for me to fix Dylan's favorite meal—rare steak and scrambled eggs. I'll chop mine up into an omelet with peppers and onions. He'll eat some of the hash browns, too.

As I set a cutting board on the counter, Dylan answers the call.

"Moen."

I can't help the giggle at his less-than-welcoming greeting, and he frowns at me. I shake my head and reach for a knife.

"Hold on. Sasha needs to hear. I'll put you on speaker."

My heart skips a beat. Oh gods! Please don't let it be Kirill's partners.

"Hello, Sasha. How are you doing?"

So lost in terrible memories, it takes a moment to realize Moen speaks to me. I clear my throat and respond I'm well. He continues.

"I spoke with the other five Alphas on the Ruling Council about Kirill and the kidnapping of unclaimed she-wolves and the turning of human females for breeding. We're going to finish what you and I started in Pennsylvania. I want to be sure you're on board to help."

Dylan lifts his gaze to me questioningly.

My stomach clenches. It's a dangerous endeavor. From the bits I learned about Garrett's findings on Kirill's computers, the network is extensive. It's in every territory. I want other females to gain their freedom. But the thought of losing Dylan makes me physically ill.

I lower my gaze and busy myself with dicing peppers.

"I want to help like I said before. But Sasha and I need to talk about it," Dylan says as he puts his hand on top of my trembling one. I lower the knife and clutch his hand.

"Understandable," Moen replies. "Which brings up another topic. Obviously, I spoke with Jagger since he's on the Ruling Council. You impressed him with your involvement and teamwork."

Dylan growls.

"Listen, Vang, hear me out. You guys were best friends for years. The challenge—regardless of your reasoning—was unnecessary. Jagger hadn't abandoned the Miami Wolves Pack when he went to Duke. Like me, he wanted to better himself to be a stronger leader. I also know how you feel about your father abandoning you. He and Jagger are not the same."

Garrett pauses to let Dylan absorb his words.

Surprisingly, he doesn't throw the mobile across the room. Instead, he closes his eyes as he pinches the bridge of his nose.

I hurry around the counter and wrap my arms around him from behind. He leans into me and sighs.

"Jagger's wedding to his fated mate—Sage—is in two days. I'm going. You should come with me and speak face-to-face with Jagger. It's been four years. Time for a fresh start."

Dylan closes his eyes again at Garrett's use of my words.

I nuzzle my fated mate's cheek.

"I hear you, Moen. I'll get back to you tomorrow," Dylan says and ends the call. He rises from the high chair and lifts me onto the counter standing between my thighs. "What do you think?"

My hands rub his bare chest, then trace his pack tattoos meaningfully.

"You chose to put these on your body, knowing tattoos are permanent. They're an indelible connection to your pack. Remember our fresh start? It's time to make amends with Jagger so you can be free of the stain caused by the challenge. His wedding is the perfect opportunity. Weddings and births signify new beginnings. Plus, I'd love to meet your mother."

I lean my forehead against his.

"But as for the network, let's think more about it. I can't lose you, Dylan Vang. You're all I have left."

He considers my words, then sighs.

"Okay. Now, you have a reason to wear that crystal evening gown you fell in love with," he says with a wry grin.

I giggle and throw my arms around his neck.

I can't wait to meet his pack. I'm sure everything will be just fine.

CHAPTER 19

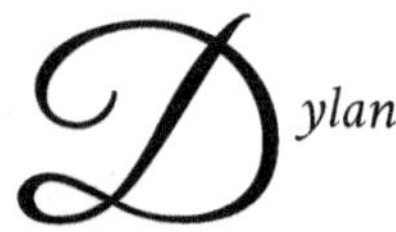ylan

"WELL, look who the cat dragged in... Dylan *The Rogue* Vang."

I bite back a snarl at Viggo's statement as I stride into the office of the clubhouse on Moon Island—the pack's private island. Jagger's younger brother smirks. His ice blue eyes flash with his red wolf. I throw a glare in his direction and stalk further into the office.

Then his lip twitches and his eyes sparkle—the jokester and playboy of the group. He leans his massive frame back in the chair and watches me, an amused expression on his face.

"Dylan."

I flick my gaze to Rust, who leans against the wall. He strikes a casual pose with his arms folded over his chest and long legs crossed at the ankles. Lean muscled and agile, we would often wrestle whenever he made a jab at me.

"Rust."

The intensity of another's stare burns into the side of my head. I know who it must be without even looking. Tag has always been the closest to Jagger. Tag's father was Alpha Marc's enforcer. A sense to protect Jagger runs high in Tag. I bet Jagger named Tag his beta.

I face him.

Green eyes flash with his brown wolf as he stands beside the current Alpha, who sits behind the desk. As I approach, Tag growls low in his chest. I ignore his warning and stride forward until I stand opposite Jagger.

"Tag."

"Dylan."

Then I turn to Jagger.

"Jagger—"

"*Alpha* to you!" Tag bites out as he folds his arms across his broad chest and widens his stance.

I snarl. Hands fisted at my sides.

"Back the fuck up, Tag! I'm not here for your bullshit."

Jagger puts up his hand and silences Tag's snarl.

"Dylan, have a seat. You requested a meeting with me. Tell me what you *are* here for."

I grind my molars at Jagger's command but sit in the leather chair in front of his desk and inhale deeply. A vision of Sasha's smiling face reminds me to use my brain, not my fists. She wants a fresh start for both of us, and I agree.

Moen's comment about my father made me realize Jagger leaving reminded me of him. Two people who I believed I could depend on abandoned me for their selfish gain. But it's not true. Jagger brought me into his circle of friends when he could have ignored my mistreatment. He stayed by my side for years no matter how bristly I behaved. I was the one who turned on him—abandoned him because of my misdirected anger. It's time to apologize. Make amends, as my fated mate told me.

A burst of happiness hits me in the chest. Sasha can sense my release of the past, and it makes her happy. I smile to myself, then raise my gaze to Jagger's ice blue one.

"I apologize for challenging you. At the time, I justified it by seeing you going to Duke as abandoning the pack. Now, I realize I misdirected anger with my father for his abandonment of my mother and me towards you. And I was wrong."

Jagger studies my face. An almost imperceptible flare of his nostrils hints he sniffs for any deceit. He narrows his eyes and rises from the chair to prowl around the desk.

I brace myself for the impact. I won't fight back because I deserve the brunt of his anger. Unlike him with mine.

He slaps me on the back, and I tense. Then he chuckles.

"Oh, you thought I was going to hit you? Damn, D., you're my brother, just much as Viggo, Tag, and Rust. I may not have gotten the paw print tattoos like the rest of you. But we can never break our connection. Yeah, you fucked up big time. But I understand why."

Jagger pulls me to my feet and gives me a bro hug. I return it with equal fierceness.

When we part, Rust claps, and Viggo lets loose with a wolf whistle. I glance at Tag. A sour expression meets my gaze. He strides forward, eyes never leaving mine. Then he grins.

"You dumb fuck! What took you so long?!"

He grabs me around the neck, and we tussle while the others laugh. I push him off and smirk.

"Didn't I tell you not to fuck with me, Tag? Don't make me open a can of whoop-ass on you right here, right now."

He and jagger glance at each other, then rush me. We fall to the floor and roll around wrestling. Viggo whoops and jumps on top of the pile. Rust chuckles.

"Listen, I'm off duty today. So, if you break bones or poke an eye out, the pack doctor is unavailable to mend you fuckers."

I scissor kick my legs to sweep his feet from underneath him. He lands on his ass with a grunt. Everyone laughs as he leaps into the fray.

Eventually, we call it a draw and sit on the floor to catch our breath.

"So, Garrett tells me you have a fated mate—"

"Shut the fuck up! Not *Mr. I Don't Believe In Fated Mates* has one? Get outta here!"

"Who the hell wants to get stuck with *you* for eternity?"

"May the gods help her…"

I roll my eyes and climb to my feet. Fuck, it feels like Viggo broke my back when he landed on us. I narrow my eyes at him, and he shrugs. Rust holds his hands up and shakes his head. I stretch and the bones snap in place with a few cracks.

"Yeah, tell me about it. That's another thing I have to admit. I walked into a diner, and my knees buckled. Her unique scent hit me upside the head, and I was a goner. Sasha Volkov, now Vang."

Jagger jumps to his feet, grinning.

"Well, I'll be damned. The tough guy met his match in a little she-wolf? Congratulations, brother!" He exclaims as he claps me on the shoulder. "Did you have a mate bonding ceremony?"

One regret I have is not giving Sasha the chance to say our vows before a pack. A rogue wolf has no one. So, who would serve as witness?

I shake my head and respond, "No. I just moved her into my penthouse and bought her everything she needed. She bears my mark, wears my ring, and goes by my name."

"What a romantic you are…" Tag shakes his head and stands. "Congratulations, anyway."

"Yeah, congrats, bro!"

"Congratulations, Dylan. I'm happy for you."

Viggo and Rust chime in and stand.

"Tonight, the pack will celebrate your mating, and you and Sasha can complete the ceremony. How does that sound?" Jagger asks.

"Thank you. But I don't want to interfere with your wedding plans—"

"No interference. Sage and I had our mate bonding ceremony. This is the wedding I promised her. In fact, you need to meet her and our twin pups, Harald and Tove. Where's Sasha?"

I tell them she's at my mother's mansion near the school. Jagger says to get them both and bring them to his bayfront mansion. We hop into golf carts and head for the residences.

~

SASHA

"LENA, you have such a lovely home. And the photos of Dylan as a boy are adorable! He's still handsome—"

"And broody!" His mother laughs.

I try not to giggle. But she smiles.

"I know my son. He loves hard and gets hurt just as hard. If someone upsets him, he lashes out. No matter who it may be, except for me, naturally. So, I'm glad he's here to speak with Jagger. I don't want Dylan to carry shame anymore—not from his father and not from the challenge."

With an understanding nod, I return her smile. She's so right. I rub my chest. So many emotions filter through our mate bond. I'm not sure how it goes after an initial decrease in tension.

I check my watch. Half an hour passed since Dylan dropped me off. At least no one has come to his mother's door demanding we get off the island. So, I guess it goes all right.

"You have a calming influence on Dylan, Sasha. He doesn't have the wildness in his eyes anymore. I don't sense his wolf so close to the surface, either. Thank you," Lena says. "I do hope he makes it right with Jagger."

As I nod in agreement, a flare of happiness comes through our bond. Then, the front door opens.

"Sasha? Mom?"

I jump to my feet and race to Dylan. He swoops me up and spins in a circle. I hold tight as he flips me to a bridal carry and strides into the living room.

"Good news! Jagger and I put the past behind us. Viggo, Tag, and Rust were there, and all's good with them, too. Of course, they ribbed me, and we wrestled. But I deserved it."

"Oh, sweetheart! I'm so happy for you!" Lena jumps to her feet clapping. Tears fill her eyes.

Dylan lowers me to stand and rushes to his mother's side. He embraces her, and they share a moment.

I watch on as tears blur my vision. This is a wonderful day! It can't get any better.

He turns to me and holds out his hand. I hurry over and clutch it between both of mine. He kisses my lips and smiles.

"And… Jagger offered the pack to celebrate you and me with a mate bonding ceremony tonight. I'm sorry I couldn't give you one as a rogue wolf. Now, you have a chance for the pack to witness our love. Do you want to do it?"

Tears stream down my cheeks as I nod vigorously. I can't believe they would be so kind!

Jagger brushes the tears with his thumb and presses his forehead to mine.

"I love you, Sasha Vang."

"I love you, Dylan Vang."

A few hours later, as the sun sets, we stand before a ceremony bower of fragrant gardenia and jasmine flowers in the middle of Moon Island beneath palm trees. The balmy air mixes with the floral aroma for a sultry scent. Whip-poor-wills chirp to welcome the night.

Dylan has on the classic black tuxedo he planned to wear to Jagger and Sage's wedding. My fated mate smiles with such love as I stand before him.

He was right. I wear the Swarovski Crystal embellished evening gown with the sparkly stilettos that complement it so well. It hugs my ass just the way he likes it.

Sage—the High Witch and leader of the powerful Coven of the South—invoked a glamour spell to apply makeup and to put soft waves in my hair. With the scar removed, the tresses flow down my back, away from my face. I smile with such jubilation in my heart.

Dylan and I exchange our mate bonding vows in front of his pack. After Jagger spoke with them, the members welcomed Dylan back into the fold. They even embraced me. Well, not the males since Dylan growled when Viggo reached for me. He didn't care and planted a kiss on my cheek, then ducked from Dylan's punch.

My heart swelled at the sight of his four best friends teasing him while he laughed. Such a lightness about him now—just as Lena mentioned. It shows in his eyes as he stares at me.

"Oh, cut it with the puppy dog eyes, D. What happened to the tough wolf shifter?"

Tag's chuckle draws our attention. He smirks and sips a glass of Champagne.

"Don't tease him, Tag. Wait until it's you who finds your fated mate," Sage says with a perfectly arched eyebrow raised. Her emerald green eyes shine with mirth.

Tag grumbles and shakes his head.

Dylan tells me he's known as the grump in the group.

"So, I guess you're moving back here now?" Garrett asks as he glances between Dylan and Jagger.

Jagger turns to us and says, "Dylan, do you plan to remain a rogue wolf, or are you bringing your ass back home?"

He chuckles and looks at me. I nod since we spoke about it earlier. I'll let Dylan answer for us. He nods back and faces Jagger and Garrett.

"Actually, Sasha has her volunteer work at the women's shelter that helped her when she first arrived in New York City. We're major donors and have a few projects in the works. And I have my MMA fighting. So, we'll live in both New York and Miami. That is if you give us permission to stay within your territory, Garrett."

I wait, praying he won't deny our request. Vera and the shelter are so important to me. I don't want to lose them. Then I sag with relief when Garrett grins and raises his Champagne flute.

"Here's to the first wolf shifter snowbirds to fly between New York and Miami, Dylan and Sasha Vang!"

Everyone around us raises their glasses as laughter fills the night.

EPILOGUE

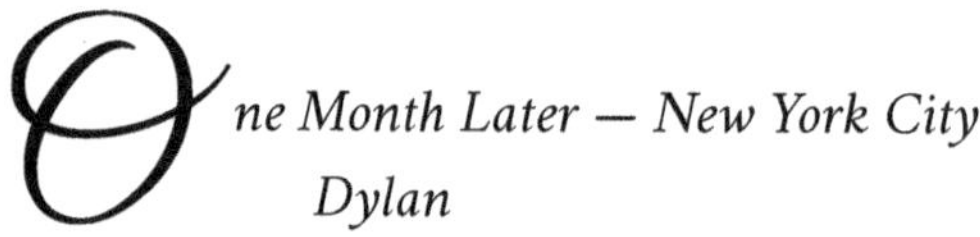

ne Month Later — New York City
Dylan

"GLAD TO HEAR Sasha made peace with her pack in Russia. It had to be hard being there after such a tragedy. Too bad you couldn't keep the land..."

As Garrett talks, I remember the sadness on her face when we drove through the forest opening to her pack's ancestral lands.

Crumbling shells of houses and buildings and melted wrecks of vehicles were all that remained after Kirill and his goons set them on fire. Scavenged by wild animals, the bodies of the fallen were long gone. Thankfully, Sasha didn't have to see any bones or remnants of clothing.

Tears spilled down her cheeks as she walked around her childhood home. She picked through some piles or rumble.

Sadly, she found nothing for keepsakes. Those fuckers did too good of a job destroying anything in their path.

We laid wreaths of fresh flowers in the center of the property. I stood by her side as she kneeled and said prayers to the gods for her family and pack. After a while, she rose, and I held her tight as she cried against my chest.

I renewed my vow to help Garrett eliminate the rest of Kirill's network. On the flight back home, I shared my decision with Sasha, and she agreed as long as I promised to put my safety first. I did. No way can I leave her alone. Well, not alone anymore since we have our Miami pack and the support of New York's pack.

Which is the reason for my visit to Garrett in his office with him and Dolph. It's amazing the last time I was here, I nearly killed Hudson. He got his later.

My thoughts drift away as I tune back in to Garrett.

"—your decision yet?"

"Yes. The trip to Sasha's pack land drove home the need to end the network. She's fine with me taking part as long as I remain safe. I promised her I would not endanger myself. So, I'm in."

Garrett nods and says, "I understand her concern and don't blame her. My enforcers trained for operations like the ones we'll face. Some are former SEALs and Green Berets. I can arrange for you to train with them. Your MMA fighting skills will come in handy. You need the weapons and tactical training. Until you're more comfortable, you won't be on point. Sounds good?"

"I'm in," I respond as I flick my gaze between Garrett and Dolph.

Both shake my hand, and I head home to my fated mate.

Before I hop on my Harley, I shoot a text message to Sasha I'm on my way. I can't wait to tell her about the training to ease her worries. As I enter our penthouse, I call out to her. Then, my wolf howls as he scratches underneath the surface of my skin, suddenly too tight for my heated body.

A sweet aroma mixed with her unique scent engulfs my senses. Every cell in my body explodes with carnal need. Immediately, my cock hardens to the point of pain. A feral howl rips from my throat as I throw my head back to inhale the aroma. The muscles of my thighs bunch as my body prepares to hurtle through our penthouse on the trail of the enthralling source.

As my feet pound on the hardwood floor, I tear out of my jacket and sweater. They drop to the floor. The zipper teeth of my jeans cut into my engorged cock. I grip the fabric and rip it apart. Only a second passes as I toe off my boots and pull the jeans down.

Buck naked, I burst through the double doors of our bedroom suite. Zoom past the sitting room and throw open the bedroom doors. My ravenous gaze scans the room.

Sasha stares at me over her shoulder as she kneels naked in the middle of the king-size bed. Mounds of pillows and blankets—from not only our bedding, but those from the guest rooms—surround her. Crimson infuses her alabaster skin from head to toe. Beads of sweat dot her forehead where strands of her hair plaster against her face. She moans pitifully and shakes her ass. Slick glistens on her inner thighs. The aroma wafts through the air.

My fated mate is in heat. Fertile and ready to bear my pup.

The sight of her is like a red flag to a bull.

I bound across the floor and pounce on the bed.

She moans as tears mingle with the sweat on her cheeks.

"D—D—Dylan... I need you. P—Please..."

Her pitiful wail as she reaches back for my cock spurs me on.

I grip her hips and angle her pelvis to line up her sopping, slick-soaked pussy with my bulbous tip. Its an angry red and shiny with pre-cum ready to plunge inside of her cunt. She lowers her forearms to the pillows and whines.

The urge to mount her hard surges my hips forward. She screams, and her pussy walls contract. Her entire body shakes violently. The force of her orgasm spirals through her.

I bellow and pump my hips like the feral beast I am. Caught in her sexual thrall, I pound her pussy with raw savagery. Mindless pleasure rolls through me as I grunt and growl. Sweat glistens on my body.

My palms smack her shapely ass, leaving red handprints on her already flushed skin.

With a throaty moan, fresh slick pours from her pussy.

The aroma increases, and my wolf loses it. We roar. More slick. Another roar and spanks to the ass trigger even more slick to coat my cock and pour down both our thighs to puddle on the piled-up bedding.

I growl and band my arm around her waist, hauling her back to my chest. I rise to my feet. Her ass rests in the cradle of my pelvis as her slippery thighs rest on top of mine. I lift her up and down, impaling her on my cock while she screams and writhes, begging me for more.

The bed frame creaks with the force of our mating. But we don't stop or slow.

Until my knot expands.

Sasha growls and claws at my arms, trying to break free as my knot stretches her wrecked pussy.

I snarl and bare my fangs. They sink into her flesh on top of my mark. I growl as her hot blood fills my mouth and shake my head, digging deeper. She keens and cums again. My thick milky seed shoots from my balls and out the slit of my cock to bathe her pussy.

"You. Will. Bear. My. Pup!"

"YEESSS!"

My legs quiver. We drop to her nest of bedding and pillows. She pants as her feverish body adjusts to my knot and her pussy pulsates. I rumble deep in my chest as my hand strokes her lower belly. Soon it will grow round with my pup. And I will have a family of my own to love. Forever.

⌇

THANK you for reading *Dylan The Rogue*!

Want to read more about the Wolves of Miami Pack and catch up with Dylan and Sasha? Read *Jagger The Temptation* and *Rust The Rejected*. Turn the page for their previews.

SUBSCRIBE to my newsletter for latest news and launches, books from my author friends, and sizzling reads in book promotions bit.ly/CLBooksJoinNewsletter.

Be sure to join my Facebook Group for a community who love my spicy worlds facebook.com/groups/charmainelouisebookscoterie!

For early access to my current works and bonus books, visit my Ream Stories reamstories.com/charmainelouisebooks.

PREVIEW JAGGER THE TEMPTATION: A WOLF SHIFTER FATED MATES PARANORMAL ROMANCE

agger

"THE QUARTERLY NUMBERS show an increase in profits. More than projected because of the opening of the beach-front resort in Charleston earlier than planned. The general manager reports the property sold out for the first four months..."

I nod as my Vice President of Hotels and Resorts for Larson Enterprises, Inc. continues his update. My mind focuses partially on his presentation.

For the last few weeks, I can't seem to focus. I don't know whether lack of sleep causes the lapse or something else. Dreams of another dominate my nights. They remain just out of reach, on the fringes. But it's their silent pleas for help that keep me tossing. A vibration from them of fear and sadness draws me closer. My instinct kicks in, and I want to save them, protect them.

Each dream brings me closer to them. But they remain just out of reach. I wake tangled in silk sheets. An arm extended as my hand reaches for them. Last night I called a name. However, as the last vestiges of the dream slipped away, the name dissolved with it.

I growl low in my chest in frustration.

My COO shifts his gaze to me. His wolf senses picked up my displeasure with ease.

I shake my head at Tag Dahl.

He cocks his head at me.

As my best friend, he's known me since we were pups. Born within a few weeks of each other—him to our pack's enforcer and me to our Alpha—Tag knows me as well as I know myself. I haven't mentioned my dreams to him, not that he'd think me nuts. No. I just don't know what they mean and if they warrant a conversation for analysis.

And Tag would delve into their meaning.

As my beta, he's my right-hand man. Anything that involves me and can impact our pack, he wants to solve the puzzle.

But this one will remain under wraps until I figure it out. So, I shake my head again and turn my attention back to the presentation. Even as I will my mind to pay full attention. I remove my personal hat. Then I firmly affix the one for my roles as CEO and Chairman of the Board of the luxury hotels, fine dining, clubs, and lounges company my family founded in Miami.

An hour later, a persistent Tag strides along with me to my suite of offices in The Larson Tower on Biscayne Bay. We pass through the executive floor as staff—wolf shifter and human—acknowledge us. The unaware humans often stare in awe at our formidable sizes. We're both six feet, seven inches of pure muscle and move with predatory grace. We nod in return but continue without pause.

I know Tag wants to find out what's up with me. I'll allow his henpecking since we're so close. Otherwise, I do not tolerate others in my business. No. One.

"Alpha, you have a few voicemails, sir."

"Thanks, Ginny," I respond to my administrative assistant as I open the double doors of my office. "Kindly hold my calls."

"What's up, Jagger?"

I bite back an irritated growl—lack of sleep will have you pissed, even at your best friend who only wants to help.

"You want a drink?" I ask as I unbutton the jacket of my bespoke three-piece Brioni suit and stride to the bar cart. It's after five-thirty, and I can use a stiff one before I head out to Club Sol & Mani for some much-needed sexual relief.

"Sure, thanks."

I take my time pouring two fingers of scotch into the Baccarat crystal tumblers. Absolutely no rush to have Tag pick at my psyche. My ears pick up his almost silent huff, and I chuckle to myself.

"Don't delay this conversation, Jag. You've been off for a few weeks now, and I've given you space," he says, then nods his thanks for the liquor. "What's up with you?"

Again, I allow him to question me, even though I'm his Alpha and my word is final.

I lower myself onto the dove gray tufted leather sofa in the seating area. Tag takes a chair opposite and places an ankle over a knee. I sip my drink as I consider my words. He knows better than to interrupt at this point.

"Dreams."

He cocks his head at the simple one-worded response. I shrug and take another sip.

"For the past few weeks, dreams invade my sleep. Every. Single. Night. Someone's in trouble. But I can't catch their name or where they are to help them," I sigh and stare out the window.

The panoramic view across Biscayne Bay with jet skiers and megayachts on its dazzling surface out to the azure Atlantic Ocean helps to quiet the inner turmoil my wolf and I sense. He turns his massive silvery white head to stare at me with accusatory ice blue eyes. It's as though he knows something I don't and pissed I'm not aware. I run my fingers through my white blond hair as I think on it, then shake my head. No clue.

"What do you recall?" Tag asks as he leans forward and places his elbows on his knees, the scotch tumbler balanced between his sizable hands.

I shrug.

"A brightness in the background prevents a clear view. I know it's outdoors since I hear the hum of insects and feel the warm sun on my skin. Naked skin. So, I must have shifted and returned to my human form."

Another sip of scotch, and I stand to pace my office.

Instinct tells me these are no ordinary dreams. But each morning I account for the whereabouts of my pack, and no one turns up missing. Not knowing who calls for my help drives me and my wolf mad.

I growl and toss back the rest of my scotch. A few long strides and I refill the tumbler.

"No one in our pack seems in trouble. I'll stop by the she-wolves' residences on my way home just to make sure. A few of our unmated males flew to New Orleans for the weekend. I'll shoot a text to them and make sure they didn't get into anything on Bourbon Street."

With a nod of agreement, I hold the decanter up. Tag declines a refill—ever the responsible one. Fine. It's not like wolf shifters can get drunk. Well, not too much. Our systems process substances differently from humans. All the better for us, especially when I'm in this pissy mood.

"Well, you know they say fated mates can have dreams about the other. The more frequent and intense they become, the closer the pair gets to their first encounter," Tag says. His emerald green eyes scan my face for a reaction. He knows I've waited all these years for my fated mate—and will continue to do so.

Despite my father's damn near daily persistence, I issue

the claiming bite and complete the mating bond with a single she-wolf. The last eleven years of nearly nonstop mating runs, with the she-wolves in my pack and those from nearby cities—hell, even overseas. Or galas at our hotels and mixers at our clubs, an accidental encounter, all to persuade me to select a she-wolf as my mate. None of them tempt me in the slightest.

All the she-wolves desire to bond with me. Then the supposed prince—and they were eager to lose their slippers and thongs for me to pick up——now the Alpha of the Miami Wolves Pack. Correction, *Billionaire Wolves of Miami* as the other packs refer to us. With good reason, since we're the most powerful pack in the South.

Several millennia ago, Scandinavian Viking wolf shifters sailed from the Old World and landed along the East Coast of what's now the United States. The six packs headed by best friends who sought new lands moved throughout the continent to form territories with ours settling here. We maintain close ties with our brethren through friendship, mating, and business. Plus, our Ruling Council gatherings keep us informed of happenings throughout the packs.

And even going that far and wide, I have yet to meet my fated mate. However, I will wait for her.

Hell, my wolf demands it as he gets agitated when he senses a she-wolf's burgeoning interest. Sure, he'll sit back while I fuck since it fills a need and doesn't equate to being mated. Wolf shifters—male and female—have strong sexual appetites. We don't have the same hang-ups as humans over casual sex, no sex before marriage, and whatever other bullshit they come up with. It's a part of our lives, just like eating or breathing. A need we won't suppress. Particularly with the built-up tension raging through my body. However, his pacing and snarls have increased recently, too.

So maybe Tag is on to something.

My *fated* mate.

A she-wolf whose scent I was born with teasing my nostrils. When she appears, I will recognize her by her distinct scent. No other will bear her uniqueness. Someday we will meet. I will give her my claiming bite, and we will have our mate bonding ceremony for all the clans to witness. I will make her mine forever.

The thought she may be in trouble makes my blood boil and my wolf snap his teeth, ears flat to his head. Our protective instinct on high alert.

So, I won't give up on finding my fated mate—or on us. No matter how many times my father bugs me about the need to bond with another. I'm no longer the teen who had to obey.

I am Alpha now.

"WE'RE HERE, ALPHA."

I glance up from my mobile screen and out the tinted window.

So focused on business emails, I didn't notice my driver

pull my Black Badge Rolls-Royce Cullinan into the driveway for Club Sol & Mani Miami. The flagship of six exclusive, luxury, members only BDSM clubs Larson Enterprises owns sits on Ocean Drive directly across from the Atlantic Ocean in a South Beach historic, beachfront gated mansion.

"Great, thank you, Cole," I respond. "I'll take it from here and will text when I'm ready to go home."

"Yes, Alpha. I'll get the door for you."

I wave him off and reach for the handle, only for the club's valet to open the door. A nod to Cole and a thanks in the form of a hundred to the young wolf shifter, and I stride to the scrolled wrought-iron and glass doors of the Spanish-style mansion. Laughter from members as they frolic in the mosaic-tiled pool within the sun-filled court-yard floats in the balmy evening air.

"Good evening, Alpha," the doorman says with a respectful bow of his head. I shake his hand and palm off another hundred. He thanks me as I move on.

"Hello, Alpha!" The two she-wolf greeters chorus cheer-fully as I walk through the opulent lobby to the elevators. Another two C-notes and I'm on the elevator headed to my personal suite.

Tonight, I'll play in privacy rather than amongst other members in Exhibition where demonstrations and perfor-mance rooms provide entertainment—or inspiration. Nor will the Dungeon do, despite my affinity for the spacious section devoted to public forms of BDSM play. Those not in the lifestyle may think it's a medieval dungeon for torture with the St. Andrew's Crosses, spanking benches, chains suspended from the ceiling, and more. To me, the pieces and assorted whips, floggers, canes, and implements are only to be expected.

The soft thrum of sensual music greets me as I step out of the elevator and into the hallway. The rhythm vibrates through my core as intended to amp arousal for what lies behind the closed doors of the eight private suites. Members can reserve them in advance should they prefer the same privacy I wish for tonight.

Each suite decorated by theme has various BDSM pieces, implements, and toys. A nice variety of options to choose from. However, my suite remains for my personal use only.

I press my palm against the plate by the door of the corner suite, and the locks disengage.

"Good evening, Alpha."

My head jerks up. What the fuck?! I allow no one in my space without my consent. My ice blue eyes adjust to the candlelit room. On my custom-built mahogany wood, king-size bed cornered by four thick carved posters and a brass lattice canopy with rings strategically attached sits a she-wolf from my pack. And not just any she-wolf. The sable-haired hellion.

"Melissa, what the fuck are you doing in my suite?!" I snarl as I stalk towards her.

She jerks back as though slapped but recovers quickly. Fully naked, she rises from the bed with the prowess of a wolf in hunt mode and slinks towards me. Amber eyes glow in the candlelight. She tosses her waist-length sable brown hair over her shoulders. Her sleek figure with high perky tits tipped by puckered rosy nipples, flat belly, narrow waist, slim hips, and long, toned legs would make any male salivate.

Not me.

Even though I planned to fuck her tonight—after I *invited* her to my suite—my stomach churns at the thought as my wolf growls low in his broad chest. He's not happy, nor am I.

Melissa is one of my regular sexual partners. We scratch the itch for each other from time to time. However, it's not like we're exclusive. Many a she-wolf join me for carnal pleasures. As Melissa has with other males. And I've made it clear I am not interested in bonding with her.

But after this stunt, this may very well be the last time I hookup with her. If she thinks she can enter my domain uninvited, she's confused. And I will speak with the club manager about her gaining unapproved access.

I have no intention of giving Melissa any ideas.

Not happening.

For one, Melissa thinks she's the alpha since the other male wolf shifters in our pack bow down to her beauty and succumb to her whims. I won't have it.

Not to mention she's a bully. Another trait I will not tolerate. I treat everyone in our pack with respect. They may not be my equal, but I don't make them feel less than.

And the most important reason... She's not my fated

mate. The only wolf shifter who will enter my domain as she pleases.

My wolf agrees with a flick of his feathery tail.

"Melissa, I have told you we fuck. Nothing more"—I raise my hand to stop her response—"You have no right to enter my personal suite without my permission. None. Get dressed. I will inform the club manager not to allow you entry ever again. This is it. Do you understand?"

She blinks, then her mouth opens.

I fold my arms over my chest and stand with feet spread far apart in a dominant manner as I pin her with an arctic gaze.

Naturally, Melissa glares back and mimics my stance as her eyes blaze golden fire.

"Jag—"

"Alpha! Alpha, Melissa. And do not forget it. We may have fucked. But you will respect me as your Alpha. Get. Dressed. And. Go. Now."

She lifts her chin in defiance, then reconsiders when I slap my sizable palm on my muscular thigh. Her eyes widen at the warning. Then she scurries to the chair and gathers her clothes to her flushed chest.

"Yes, Alpha!" She exclaims.

With a stern eye, I watch as she dresses quickly.

Melissa stops at the door and glances at me over her shoulder. Her oval-shaped face pinched with worry. She knows she took it too far this time.

"Sorry, Alpha," she whispers, then opens the door and leaves.

I sigh and sink onto the bed.

Well, there goes the idea of releasing tension. More just built up.

With his tongue hanging out from the side of his mouth, my wolf yips. Ice blue eyes gleam with mirth. It's as though he laughs at my misfortune.

I growl at him and slump back on the navy blue silk pillows. My thoughts drift to my conversation with Tag. Perhaps fate doesn't want me with another since my mate will appear soon. My eyes close on a sigh.

Where are you?

~

Click the Image Below or Visit books2read.com/u/ mZEL2e For Your Copy

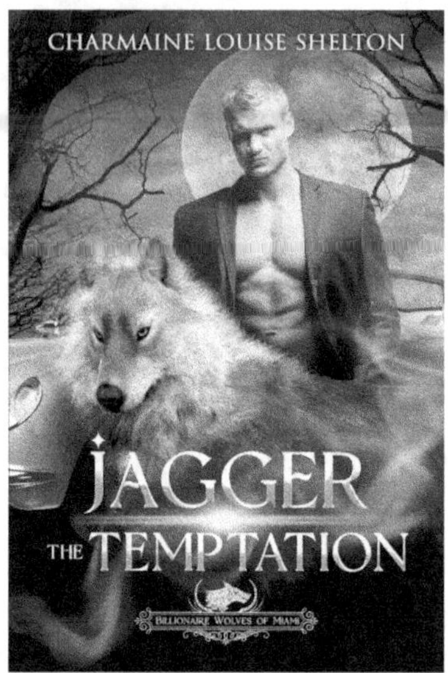

Jagger The Temptation: A Wolf Shifter Fated Mates Paranormal Romance

ust

"Oh, my, Dr. Ingolf. What a big stethoscope you have, Sir. So long and hard. Ooo and look! It even has a shiny tip. Shall I blow on it to warm it for you, Sir?"

The submissive purses her full glossy lips as she stares up at me from the velvet pillow between my feet. A rich chocolate brown rims her dilated pupils.

But it's the sight of her pillowy tits overflowing the cups of her pink lace corset that makes my cock leak pre-cum. The perfect size to fit in my large hands and soft. Nothing against silicone enhancements, but the feel of naturally lush tits with pinchable plump nipples wins.

My mouth salivates as much as my cock drips.

The Alpha Dom in me knows I should correct the

sub's forward behavior. I did not command her to fist my dick—only to kneel. Any other time, I would toss her over my thighs and spank her round ass. The globes on either side of the skimpy lace thong would match its color for a delightful rosy shade. My palm itches for the punishment.

Instead, I sigh and pinch the bridge of my nose—not a nipple.

I've had back-to-back nights as a critical care surgeon at Miami's busiest hospital emergency room. The urban location has more than its share of acute, life-threatening injuries that require immediate surgery. Trained to perform well under pressure, I never hesitate to pick up the scalpel to save a patient.

My duties require the utmost focus. I cannot allow distractions. A patient's life—many times their heart—is in my hands, literally.

So, when I have a rare night off from the ER and no one in our pack needs Dr. Ingolf, I don't waste it. I take advantage of the opportunity to revel in my dominate proclivities.

A trip to Club Sol & Mani Miami provides a safe space for those in the BDSM lifestyle. The luxury, members-only club on Ocean Drive owned by the Miami Wolves Pack promises a night of pleasure.

I let my gaze return to the sub. She winks at me. Uh. No.

"Oh, naughty pet, how you misbehave," I tsk as I tuck my cock back into my bespoke trousers and zip up. Her mouth droops in dismay. "I must let the resident Dom know you like to top from the bottom."

Her glossy lips pout as elegantly shaped eyebrows pinch together and mar her pretty face. The little she-wolf even dares to growl at my reprimand.

Well, damn. That will never do.

She yelps as I scoop her from the pillow and over my muscular thighs. Long blonde hair falls over her face like a silky curtain. Her hands scrabble for the floor while her shapely legs flail.

I trap them with one of mine and press a hand between her shoulder blades to still her movements. A deep growl of my own halts her wiggling. Then a swat to her left ass cheek makes her jolt.

"Enough with this, naughty pet. You will take your punishment like a well-trained Club Sol & Mani sub. Twenty spanks, and you will count each one. Miss one, and we start anew. Do you understand?"

She shivers as I add Alpha power to my words. The musky scent of her arousal flares. I inhale deeply. My cock throbs, and my wolf howls. Yeah, it's been a while.

"Yes, Sir. I apologize and will behave appropriately."

I smirk as my palm rubs the soft skin of her upturned ass. A moan slips past her lips, and her pelvis tilts to push her ass into my hand.

THWACK.

"You disobey during a punishment?"

Her ass lowers as she shakes her head. Blonde strands sway with the light catching the golden streaks.

"Words, naughty pet. I will have your words."

"N—No, Sir."

"Count, or we start from one."

"One, Sir." She replies immediately.

Halfway through, the intoxicating scent of her arousal permeates the air in my private suite. A damp patch of it spreads through the wool of my trousers. I rim her slick pussy lips with the calloused tip of my middle finger.

She gasps, and her greedy core clenches. Then she wails when I issue three successive spanks to her swollen folds. But she doesn't miss the count.

I thrust two tapered fingers inside of her pussy. It pulsates around the digits, sucking them in deep. So tight and wet. I stifle a groan. Too damn long.

"Twenty, Sir."

The sub ends on a choked pant.

I lift her to straddle my lap.

Tears stream down her reddened cheeks. Like her ass, they bear a crimson shade. I pull the Ferragamo silk pocket square from my suit jacket and dab her face. Chocolate brown eyes now softened lower to stare at my chest submissively.

"You did well, pet. Now, you will think twice before topping a Dom. Won't you?" I ask with a cocked eyebrow.

"Thank you, Sir. Yes, I will," she whispers.

"Good. Now, we fuck," I say as my hands cup her heated ass, and I rise. Quick strides take me to the sex swing. Even quicker, I strap her in.

Excitement shines in her eyes, even as she keeps them

lowered. Her teeth nibble at the corner of her mouth. Dainty fingers wrap around the black suede straps. Her thighs—slick with her juices—quiver in anticipation.

She doesn't have long to wait.

I unzip my trousers, and my aching cock springs free. It slaps back against my shirt. The engorged mushroom tip reaches my belly button. I slip a condom over it.

Teeth marks dimple her lip as she moans at the sight of my dick.

I fist its wide base and stroke up the veiny shaft once, squeezing below the head. Pearly beads of pre-cum drip to floor. Her lust-filled eyes follow their descent. Then snap to my face when I grab her hips and pull.

The sex swing arcs forward. We watch as her pussy swallows the length and girth of my cock. The tip parts her glistening folds, then disappears inch by delicious inch into her soaked core. When my heavy balls meet her heated ass cheeks, we groan in unison.

My eyes close. The sensation of tight, wet warmth clamping on my dick makes my balls tingle. Finally. Fuuuck. I relish the moment before I withdraw to my tip.

The sub mewls in protest at the loss.

"Oh, little pet, I will satisfy you many times over. But you will not cum until I give you permission. Do you understand?"

"Yes, Sir, thank you, Sir!"

I chuckle wickedly and pull the sex swing forward to plunge back in. With each arc of the swing, her pussy flutters around my cock. Too much and I draw back, edging her until she begs to cum.

The forceful thrusts pop her tits from the corset. I lean over and suckle the plump nipples. She moans as her inner walls clench around my cock. A few more thrusts, and my control hangs on by a thread.

"Now, pet! Keep cumming until I give you permission to stop," I growl.

She keens as her first orgasm causes her body to buck in the sex swing.

I grunt and growl as I fuck her through one wave after the other of her toe-curling orgasms until she's limp in the swing. Then I chase my release with a roar to the ceiling. My knees turn to jelly, and my still erect cock slips from her pussy.

She whimpers.

I tuck my junk away, then uncuff her from the sex swing and carry her to the bed. With a sated sigh, she rolls to her side, curled up like a well-fed pup. I chuckle to myself as head to the en suite bathroom for a warm, moistened cloth and clean her gently. I apply a soothing salve to her warm crimson ass cheeks, and she moans softly. Tucked beneath the silk sheets, I leave the contented she-wolf with a note beside her pillow to stay the night and enjoy breakfast.

I skip the shower and go downstairs to my McLaren P1 LM. The ride to my bayfront mansion on our pack's Moon Island in Biscayne Bay brings me back to reality.

I let my mind wander as I drive along Collins Avenue,

South Beach in my rearview mirror. And as my thoughts have in recent months, they go to what I long for to complete my life. No matter how successful I am in the ER or how many—or how few—nights at Club Sol & Mani, one thing still eludes me.

My fated mate…

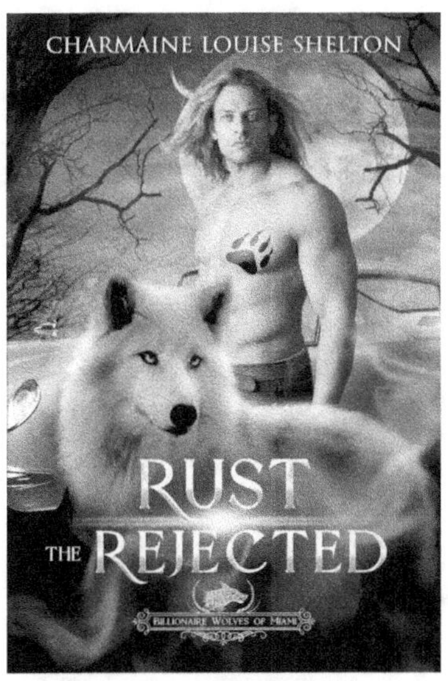

**Rust The Rejected: A Wolf Shifter Rejected Mate
Paranormal Romance**

ALSO BY CHARMAINE LOUISE SHELTON

STEELE INTERNATIONAL, INC.

A BILLIONAIRES ROMANCE SERIES

<u>Discover My Desires Sebastian & Lola Prequel</u>
(Available Exclusively to Subscribers)

<u>Fulfill My Desires Sebastian & Lola Part I</u>

<u>Heighten My Desires Sebastian & Lola Part II</u>

<u>Gift My Desires Sebastian & Lola First Christmas</u>

<u>Ignite My Desires Roger & Leonie Part I</u>

<u>Stoke My Desires Roger & Leonie Part II</u>

<u>Justify My Desires Roger & Leonie Part III</u>

<u>Deepen My Desires Sebastian & Lola Part III</u>

<u>Capture My Desires Malcolm & Starr Part I</u>

<u>Embrace My Desires Malcolm & Starr Part II</u>

<u>Cherish My Desires Malcolm & Starr Part III</u>

<u>A Trilogy of Desires Sebastian & Lola Parts I-III</u>

<u>A Trilogy of Desires Roger & Leonie Parts I-III</u>

<u>A Trilogy of Desires Malcolm & Starr Parts I-III</u>

<u>Series Extras</u>

<u>Series Playlist</u>

STEELE INTERNATIONAL, INC. - JACKSON CORPORATION

A BILLIONAIRES ROMANCE SERIES CROSSOVER

<u>Tempt My Desires Lachlan & Haley Part I</u>

<u>Tease My Desires Lachlan & Haley Part I</u>

<u>Grant My Desires Lachlan & Haley Part III</u>

<u>Intrigue My Desires Harris & Kat Part I</u>

<u>Decode My Desires Harris & Kat Part II</u>

<u>Honor My Desires Harris & Kat Patt III</u>

<u>A Trilogy of Desires Lachlan & Haley Parts I-III</u>

<u>A Trilogy of Desires Harris & Kat Parts I-III</u>

<u>Series Extras</u>

<u>Series Playlist</u>

BILLIONAIRE WOLVES SERIES

WOLF SHIFTER FATED MATES PARANORMAL ROMANCE

MIAMI

Jagger The Awakening

(Available Exclusively to Subscribers)

Jagger The Temptation

Rust The Rejected

Tag The Redemption

Viggo The Obsession

Dylan The Rogue

Billionaire Wolves of Miami — The Complete Collection

NEW YORK

Signy's Mates

Signy Claimed

Signy Forever

Series Playlist

Complete List bit.ly/CharmaineLouiseSheltonBooksList

CharmaineLouiseBooks.com

To read her current works in progress, visit her Ream Stories reamstories.com/charmainelouisebooks.

ABOUT CHARMAINE LOUISE SHELTON

Charmaine Louise Shelton loves a dominant Alpha hero—human, shifter, or vampire—as long as he's a billionaire and sexy as sin! Her romance novels take readers into the heroes' glitzy, glamorous, steamy worlds as they chase after independent women who unexpectedly capture their hearts.

Want to experience some more? Follow her on social media on your favorite channels below. Read her current works in progress at her Ream Stories bit.ly/Charmaine LouiseBooksCoterie. Join her newsletter for the latest updates, releases, and more bit.ly/CLBooksJoinNewsletter.

Find her at:
CharmaineLouiseBooks.com

Fulfill Your Desires.

BB bookbub.com/authors/charmaine-louise-shelton

tiktok.com/@authorcharmainelouise

youtube.com/@charmainelouisebooks

facebook.com/CharmaineLouiseBooks

instagram.com/charmainelouisebooks

goodreads.com/charmainelouisebooks

DEDICATION

To my awesome and dedicated beta readers and ARC Team, my amazing author friends, and this incredible community for their support.

And most of all to you, my loyal readers who love these couples as much as I do.

Thank you!

Fulfill Your Desires.

xoxo
Charmaine Louise Shelton